LOVE

DISCARD

ALSO BY MICHELLE A. VALENTINE

The Black Falcon Series
Rock the Beginning
Rock the Heart
Rock the Band
Rock My Bed
Rock My World
Rock the Beat
Rock My Body

Hard Knocks Series
Phenomenal X
Xaiver Cold

The Collectors Series
Demon at My Door
Coming Soon—Demon in My Bed

A Sexy Manhattan Fairytale
Naughty King
Fiesty Princess
Dirty Royals

Wicked White Series
Wicked White
Wicked Reunion
Wicked Love

A WICKED WHITE NOVEL

MICHELLE A. VALENTINE

Published by Montlake Romance, Seattle

www.apub.com

Amazon, the Amazon logo, and Montlake Romance are trademarks of Amazon.com, Inc., or its affiliates.

ISBN-13: 9781503935457
ISBN-10: 1503935450

Cover design by Jason Blackburn

Printed in the United States of America

AVERY

While the moonlight dances off the shiny red paint of his tricked-out sports car, my blood boils, turning my face the same shade as his car. How could he? And with *Charity Bidwell*, of all people?

Reality hits hard that I'm being cheated on. It smacks me right in my face. There's no denying it this time. My first instinct is to burst out in tears like a little girl whose puppy was just run over, but I can't do that—not with my sorority sister, Sasha, sitting in the driver's seat. She'd never let me live it down. I'm supposed to be tough. I'm Kappa Kappa Gamma, for crying out loud. I can't allow a jerk like Chance Murphy to make me the laughingstock of Ohio State's campus just as I'm finally accepted into the Greek life.

"Well, Avery?" Sasha smirks with her I-told-you-so face. "What are you going to do about that?"

"Yeah, *Avery*. Are you going to let him get away with that shit?" Rosemary, another one of my sisters, chimes in from the backseat while checking her makeup in the rearview mirror.

They want action. They came with me tonight just to get firsthand gossip, so I have to give people something to talk about—something that'll make the rest of the sorority forget the fact that Chance was in Highland Cinema sucking face with Charity, making me look like a pathetic loser in the process.

The muscles in my neck tense at the thought of people laughing at me on Monday morning, so I push my fingers into the tight flesh on the back of my neck and sigh. I close my eyes, trying to plan my move, and the only thing I can think of is revenge. I want to hurt him the way he has hurt me. My eyes snap open as my plan unfolds in my brain. The one thing Chance loves is that car—that pretty, red sports car that's mocking me with its presence. The one that's sitting all alone at the far end of the parking lot and begging for punishment.

"Pop your trunk," I order Sasha.

With lightning-quick speed I fling open the car door and hop out of the car. Behind me, Sasha and Rosemary giggle as they exit the car and make their way over to me while I riffle through Sasha's trunk. My heart pounds in my chest as the image of what I'm about to do to that car replays over and over in my brain.

"What are you looking for?" Sasha quizzes as she flicks her long brown hair over her shoulder and studies my movements.

My hand lands on cold hard steel and I pull it out of the trunk for a better look. "This."

"What the hell is that?" Rosemary asks as she leans in for a closer look, her green eyes dancing with excitement as her ruby-red lips twist in confusion.

The laugh that escapes my mouth startles me a little, because it doesn't even sound like me. It has the ring of someone thinking very dark and menacing things, not feeling heartbroken, like I really feel now. I'm pretty sure this is a sign that I'm losing my mind, but it's too late to turn back now. These girls will never let me live it down if I don't take some kind of action. "It's a crowbar."

Sasha smiles, clearly pleased with my revenge plot. "Nice."

Rosemary, on the other hand, still seems confused by the wicked plan going on in my mind. "What a minute, Avery. You can't possibly use that on them."

I roll my eyes and slam the trunk lid. "Rosemary, it's not to hurt them with."

Rosemary scrunches her face. For being the so-called brains of our group, she isn't always the brightest crayon in the box. Our little secret society really needs to adjust what they view as brilliance and stop giving so much credit to girls who sleep their way onto the dean's list.

I take off toward the bright red show-of-money that's shining under the glow of the street lamps, planning to reciprocate the pain I feel. The steel now feels warm in my grip, after taking some of the built-up heat from my sweaty palm, nearly matching my body temperature.

This is the last time I'll allow myself to be hurt like this. I'm sick of men treating me like something they can use, then toss away.

I stop in front of the red Camaro and zero in on the headlights as I raise the crowbar above my head.

"What in the hell do you think you're doing?" a deep voice asks from behind me, halting me instantly in my tracks.

I spin around and my eyes land on possibly the hottest guy I've ever seen. My mouth falls agape as the stranger, who doesn't appear to be much older than me, stares at me through narrowed eyes. I swallow hard as I take in the tattoos covering both of his bulging forearms and snaking up the exposed skin on his chest that's visible through the V-neck of his white T-shirt. His blond hair, a bit on the longish side, swoops across his forehead, creating a frame to show off his light blue eyes while the five-o'clock shadow he's sporting on his chiseled jaw gives him a rugged edge. This guy is absolutely gorgeous in that badass, I'll-break-your-heart-after-I've-melted-your-panties kind of way, but there's something lingering in his eyes that makes him seem like he could be sweet even though his outward appearance screams trouble.

As gorgeous as he may be, my first instinct is to tell him to piss off and to mind his own damn business, but the expression on his face lets me know that it probably won't fly well with him. He doesn't look like the type of guy that does well with someone trying to push him around.

So, I decide the truth might be the best bet in this situation. It's not like what I'm about to do isn't totally obvious. "I'm about to smash my lying, cheating boyfriend's headlights in, and if you don't mind, I would like to get back to it before he comes out here and catches me."

Tattooed hottie quirks one of his eyebrows, and his lips twist into an amused expression. "Brutal honesty. I like it. It's just a shame to fuck up such a beautiful ride, but it sounds like this douche bag has it coming if he's cheating on a smokin' chick like you. By all means—" He flips his hand over, palm out. "—please, continue."

"Thank you," I say and then turn my attention back to the car, completely delighted to get back to taking my rage out on Chance's car.

I raise my hands back in the air, gripping the steel tightly. The stares of all the witnesses weigh down on me. What I'm about to do is a crime, and I'm now having second thoughts about going through with wrecking his car. Sasha and Rosemary are supposed to be my friends, but I know they only hang out with me out of obligation. It wouldn't take much convincing for them to rat me out.

If I get caught, I could get into a lot of trouble for this, and is it really worth it? Is Chance worth it?

The short answer to that is no, and as much as I want to save my budding reputation, I can't stand the thought of disappointing my father—the one person who believes in me the most in this world.

I lower my hands, allowing the crowbar to hang at my side.

"What are you doing, Avery? Come on! We came here for a show," Sasha complains.

I turn around and face her and then shrug. "I can't do it."

She rolls her eyes and then turns toward Rosemary. "God. She's such a loser. I told you guys that she wasn't Kappa Kappa material. Let's get out of here."

I open my mouth to fire back a snippy rebuttal, but I don't get a chance. Both girls turn on their heels and rush back to Sasha's car. The engine fires up once they are inside, and soon all I see is the taillights of the little black Porsche we all came here together in. I stand there watching my ride leave me behind, with a crowbar in my hands, in the parking lot with a complete stranger. Alone. To make matters worse, my purse is in Sasha's car, so I'm stuck here with no phone and no money.

How in the hell am I supposed to get back to the house now?

My shoulders slump as I glance around the dark parking lot. I can't believe they left me here. Some best friends they are.

"Nice friends." As if Hottie McHotterson wasn't already reading my mind, he adds, "Looks like you need a ride."

I spin around on my heel to face him. "That's generous of you, but I don't get into cars with strangers."

"Just assholes and bitches then?" he asks, mildly amused.

"Excuse me?" I snap.

He shrugs. "I was just stating the obvious fact that you are a poor judge of character. You won't accept a ride from a Good Samaritan, but you'll date a guy that treats you like shit and be friends with girls who leave you stranded in a dark parking lot with a man who you don't know. Like I said, poor judge of character."

"You know what, screw you, buddy." I don't like the way this guy is able to call me out within five minutes of meeting me, no matter if what he's saying is true or not.

"I'm not the one screwed here, sweetheart."

Ugh. This guy is infuriating and could use a dose of manners. "You really need to work on your people skills. That's not how you talk to people."

5

He chuckles. "I don't seem to be the one with poor people skills. I'm not the one stranded, remember."

"Just because you have a car doesn't mean people don't think you're an asshole," I fire back.

Frustrated with this entire situation, and the fact that my still being here puts me at risk of Chance coming out and discovering me, I decide it's time to end this argument.

I stalk past Mr. Tattoo without saying another word.

"I wouldn't go that way if I were you. It's not exactly safe," he calls to me.

That halts me in my tracks. While I'm not exactly a wuss, I'm not the strongest girl in town either. I pride myself on being more of a runner to keep in shape versus someone who uses weights.

"Come on," he says with a smile. "I promise that I'm a perfect gentleman."

While I know accepting a ride from this guy is absolutely one of the worst ideas I've ever had, my only other option is to wait for Chance and explain what I'm doing here and ride in a car with him and Charity.

No fucking thank you.

I would rather take my chances with the rough part of town, or even worse, with a beautiful tattooed stranger who seems willing to help.

"Fine," I huff. "I'll go with you, but I'm keeping the crowbar. If you try anything with me, I swear I won't think twice before I beat you to a pulp with it."

"Nothing will happen to you. Scout's honor." He smirks and holds up three fingers. "Come on. I'm just over here."

He turns and heads in the direction of a beat-up, old pickup truck that's covered in mud. Without another word of protest I trail behind him, squeezing the crowbar in my hands. I have to admit this isn't the smartest thing I've ever done, but I'm desperate to get out of here, and desperate people do crazy things.

The old rusted door creaks on its hinges when he opens it, and then he stretches out his hand toward me. "It's kind of a high step. I'll help you in." I hesitate and stare down at his hand, unsure if I'm willing to loosen the death grip both of my hands have on the piece of steel.

He notices my hesitation and nods. "Look, I know we're strangers, but I promise you I'm not some weird psychopath. You can trust me."

I raise my brows. "Trust you? I don't even know your name and I'm supposed to *trust* you?"

Tattooed hottie grimaces. "My bad. I thought I introduced myself." He turns his right hand over for the customary handshake. "I'm Tyler Mercer."

My right hand releases the bar and I take his hand. The minute his warm skin touches mine, tingles shoot over me. In some strange way I instantly feel connected to this guy and become a little more at ease. "Avery Jenson."

A smile passes over Tyler's face. "It's nice to meet you, Avery. Now hop your ass in the truck so I can take you home."

I nod and then slide into the truck with Tyler's help. Once he closes me inside, I notice how clean the truck is. It's not what I expected, judging from the dirty outside of the vehicle.

When Tyler slides into the driver's seat, he fires up the truck before turning to me. "Where to?"

"Ohio State campus—no, wait." The thought of facing my sorority sisters after this botched attempt at revenge isn't something I feel like doing tonight. I need to go somewhere I feel safe, and right now only one place comes to mind. "Can you take me home to New Albany?" I ask him. "I don't feel like showing my face at the sorority house."

He stares at me for a brief moment and then nods. "Sure thing."

Tyler pulls onto the road and heads toward the freeway. "So those girls who were with you . . . they're your sorority sisters?"

I sigh. "Yes."

"So what are you studying?"

"I haven't declared a major."

His gaze flicks to me. "Don't most people in college have a specific thing to study?"

I shrug. "I don't really know what I want to be yet."

Tyler nods. "Fair enough. That's the main reason I didn't go to college. Figured it would be a waste of money if I took classes with no real goal."

"My dad doesn't really see it that way. Education is a big deal for him."

We exit the freeway and then I direct Tyler through the city streets to my house. He pulls up in front of the two-story brick colonial. It's odd there's not one single light on. This late in the evening, I was sure Dad would be home, but there's not even a porch light on outside. Given all the things that have been going on with my family lately, Dad usually doesn't leave the house much.

"Wow," Tyler says as he stares at my house. "Your house is amazing. It's like a mansion or something."

That's the reaction a lot of people have when they see my family's home. It's the biggest house in this upscale neighborhood, but what people don't know is it's also a representation of a life that I'll no longer be living before long.

"Well, thanks for the ride." I open the door and hop out, but before I close the door, I turn and add, "Maybe I'll see you around."

His face lights up. "Hopefully. Take care, crowbar."

I shake my head and roll my eyes as I shut the door and head up the sidewalk toward the house. Tyler's truck roars to life as he drives off.

Even though this started off as a completely shitty night, meeting Tyler definitely made things a lot better. He was nice eye candy to have in front of me to take my mind off Chance.

It's just too bad that I'll never see him again.

AVERY

The second I step foot into Chance's frat house, I immediately regret my decision to come to the party and face him after nearly bashing up his car last night, but it's pretty much required that all the ladies of Kappa Kappa attend this mixer. I don't know why the Greek societies make such a big deal out of following tradition on everything when all events are just excuses to party anyhow.

This just happens to be the party of the year.

Everyone is here, well, okay, not *everyone*, because we won't let just anyone into our social functions, but everyone in the Greek societies is here. These are my friends, okay, maybe *friends* isn't the right word because that's stretching it. I'm not really that close to any of these people. We're merely equals in the grand circle of Ohio State's social scene.

The live band playing bangs out the last few notes of the song as I reach the kitchen. Male bodies surround the keg but part when I come up, giving me access to get my drink.

A particularly cute guy with curly brown hair smiles as he hands me the tap. "Ladies first."

Seems the word about my crazy antics yesterday hasn't reached everyone yet. The guys are still being civil to me.

"Thanks." I smile as I fill up a red plastic cup and then turn back toward the crowded living room where the band is playing.

My hips rock in time with the beat of the fast song being played, but I refuse to get too out of control and draw a lot of attention to myself. I just want to blend in with everyone else who is having a good time in here.

It doesn't take long before I recognize the feisty song that's now being given a rock twist by the band. These guys are good. Maybe even the best band we've ever had play at one of our events.

The flimsy red cup in my hand is full of my drink of choice—a plain old beer—as I stretch my neck to get a better look at the band through the crowd. For some reason guys like it when a girl chooses a non-girlie drink, so that's what I always go for.

When my eyes zero in on the guys on the makeshift stage in the corner of the living room, my breath catches the moment my gaze fixes on a familiar face. It's Tyler—the guy who saved me last night—and he's just as sexy as I remember him. Tall, lean, with shaggy, dark blond hair. Intricate tattoos cover his impressive forearms and the black wifebeater tank top he has on shows off his sculpted chest and broad shoulders. He's the epitome of a rock star. I don't know why it didn't hit me last night that Tyler was more a rocker type versus the crazy guy I first took him for. This explains his bad-boy appearance.

It's then that I notice his eyes. They appear even bluer than they did last night, if that's possible. I stand there awestruck, unable to tear my gaze away from this breathtaking man in front of me.

Tyler pulls the microphone up to his full lips and sings the chorus of the song. His eyelids close, and the moment feels almost sensual, like I'm witnessing him baring his soul. His voice is as smooth as a silk ribbon sliding against my skin. It's hypnotic and beautiful with a bit of rasp that turns it downright sexy.

He's unbelievably hot—hotter even than last night. There's just something about a man who commands the stage that's undeniably sexy.

I push myself up to the front of the crowd, needing a closer look at the guy I haven't stopped thinking about since he dropped me off outside my house. I had mentally prepared myself to never see him again, so seeing him again is a bit of a surprise.

Tyler opens his eyes and then flicks his gaze down to me, effectively pinning me in place. Our eyes connect and a slow, sexy grin spreads across his face.

I bite my bottom lip, but it doesn't stop me from smiling like an idiot. It's nice to be noticed, especially from a guy who looks like him. It's also nice that his expression gives away that he remembers me too.

The rhythmic melody of the song has me nearly in a trance as I stare openly at Tyler while he continues to sing the song and strum the guitar in front of him. Watching his fingers move with ease causes a wicked thought to pop into my head.

Bet he's pretty good with those fingers in other areas too.

A blush creeps over my face as I think dirty thoughts about my savior, and I'm glad that people in the room don't have the ability to hear someone else's thoughts because I would simply die from embarrassment if he knew what I was thinking right now.

When the last few beats of the song play, he glances back down at me and winks, causing my blush to deepen even more.

The crowd bursts out in cheers and everyone turns their attention to Tyler. He grins and says into the microphone, "Thank you guys so much! We're Purple Haze and we're just getting started for you! I'm going to turn the lead vocals over to Jimmy here—" Tyler points to a guy who looks more like a hipster than a rocker in his black skinny jeans and flannel shirt. Jimmy rakes his long bangs back out of his face, causing me to notice that one side of his dark hair is completely buzzed while the rest is shaggy. It's a very edgy look. Jimmy jumps up from behind the drums and stalks toward the front of the stage. "—Be nice to him, ladies!"

Catcalls erupt all around and I join in by screaming along with the rest of the people in the house as Jimmy steps forward to the center of the stage. Tyler takes Jimmy's place back on the drums and he looks just as comfortable back there as he does center stage.

"Are you ready to party?! Tyler, kick that beat, man!" Jimmy commands, and the music instantly fires into another fast song.

Tyler's muscles stretch beneath his tattooed skin as he pounds on the drums, and it draws my attention to his large biceps.

I tuck a loose strand of my dark hair back behind my ear and nod my head to the beat. Most guys I know really only excel at one thing, but Tyler seems to be the exception to that rule. Not only can he sing, but he can play the drums like crazy! It appears he's a man of many talents after all.

I throw back a gulp of my bitter yellow drink when Charity, my archnemesis, comes strolling up with a smirk on her face. I can't wait to hear what's about to come out of her mouth. She's here to no doubt brag about her date with Chance.

Charity has never really made any attempt to hide her contempt for me for dating Chance. I was warned by my other sisters to stay away from Chance because he dated Charity when they were both freshmen, but seeing as that was nearly three years ago, I honestly didn't think Charity would care. I even asked her if she was okay with it before I started dating him three months ago. She told me that Chance was no longer on her radar and that I could have him if I wanted him.

Guess she really didn't mean that after all or else she wouldn't have been out with him last night.

To complicate things even more, Charity is the president of our Kappa Kappa Gamma. She prides herself on our house being known as the well-off Greek house on campus, because we only accept pledges whose families have a certain number of zeros attached to their bank accounts. A practice I've always been totally against, but that doesn't seem to matter much to anyone else but me.

"I can't believe you have the nerve to show your face here," Charity taunts. "If I were you, I would've killed myself."

"If you think I care about you and Chance, you're wrong." I do my best to stand there and pretend that what she just said doesn't hurt like hell. It's hard knowing that the people who are supposed to be your friends are so catty.

So much for the unbreakable bond of sisterhood.

She might be the president, but I don't have to take her bashing me whenever she feels like it. I have always stood up to her, even in situations when no one else would. It's because I won't go along with everything she says that she doesn't like me. I know it.

This whole Chance thing is just a way for her to get back at me, but I want to make sure she knows that she still doesn't intimidate me.

I square my shoulders and meet her gaze head-on. "If you're waiting on me to break down and cry over the fact that you went out with Chance last night, you can go away right now. That's not going to happen."

Through the loud music, mock screeching and hissing sounds commence from the crowd around us. I turn and find Chance standing in the middle of a group of guys watching Charity and me intently. They're no doubt waiting on a catfight to occur. The noises cease when I practically shoot daggers out of my eyeballs at Chance. He immediately shuts up and smacks the guys on either side of him so they'll do the same.

"No. It's not *me* who needs to go away. *You're* no longer welcome." Charity smirks.

I do my best to turn and ignore her, but I can't help firing back a retort. "Fuck off, Charity. You can't kick me out of the Kappa Kappa because you're jealous over me and Chance."

"He has nothing to do with it. The house took a vote since the news of what your father did was splashed all over the press and decided you being one of us isn't sending out the right message of what we're about."

I roll my eyes and try to fight back showing how much that fucking stings. I can't believe they are holding that shit against me. I'm sure not all the sisters feel this way. They have to know that the incident doesn't represent the kind of person I am.

I lift my cup toward my lips to put on the act that I'm not fazed in the slightest by Charity and what she says. Before the drink touches my mouth, I feel fingers wrap around my wrist and jerk it, spilling my beer all over my shirt.

The nerve!

My nostrils flare as I slam the cup down on the floor. "You bitch!"

"Oh, I'm sorry." Charity laughs as she covers her mouth in mock shock with her perfectly manicured hand. "Well, I guess you'll have to go to the thrift store and get yourself another shirt. I'm sure your family can still afford to shop there."

My jaw starts to ache from my clenched teeth. I want to hit her. I want to scream. I've tried for the past couple of months to forget—I had to, forgetting is the only way I've made it—but Charity rubbing my family's tragedy in my face is more than I can take.

My life is crumbling because of the stupid mistake my father made, and I hate that everyone now knows about it.

I'll admit when I first learned my dad was a thief, I wanted to crawl in a hole somewhere, shrivel up, and die. What girl wants to learn her dad stole almost a million dollars while he was the chief financial officer at McMullen's Candy, a major corporation? Not me. Thank God he struck a deal with the cops and his company to stay out of jail. Don't get me wrong, I'm glad he didn't go to prison, but his whole mess has completely turned my life into a living hell.

I open my mouth to fire back at Charity, but she's right. I no longer belong here. I can't afford it.

Reality hits me hard, and the emotion I've worked so hard to hide comes out in full, embarrassing force.

Tears stream down my face, and Charity folds her arms across her chest while wearing a smug grin. "Now leave. Kappa Kappa Gamma no longer needs you."

A crushing weight slams down on my heart. Being a part of this sorority was the one little piece of normalcy I had left, and now that's being taken away along with everything else that's been a constant in my life.

I spin around and notice most of the eyes in the room are zeroed in on me, and the overwhelming need to get out of here overtakes me. A sob rips through me as I turn and run out of the room. A ruckus behind me ensues as the music stops, but I don't dare turn back to see what's going on.

I have to get out of here.

I burst through the front doors, and the cool night air kisses the bare skin on my shoulders, causing me to shiver. People milling about in front of the house stare at me like I've grown three heads and sprouted a tail, and they quickly move away from me, probably worried I'm about to puke on their shoes.

I step out onto the grass and shove my hair back off my face while my breath comes out in little white puffs into the darkness. I focus on my breathing and try to calm myself down so I don't completely lose my head in front of all these strangers.

"Avery? You okay?" a deep, familiar voice asks from behind me.

I suck in a breath and swat away the tears that continue to stream down my cheeks. I can't bear to turn around and look at him. Twice now Tyler has witnessed me in some embarrassing situation. Twice now he's been the one to make sure I'm all right. How sad is my life that a complete stranger is the one who's been comforting me? I have no real friends. The only person on the face of this planet who cares about me is my father and he's now a known criminal.

"Avery?" The concern in Tyler's voice is clear. "Talk to me."

My heart pounds as I turn to face him. His eyes soften as soon as he spots my face and he takes a tentative step toward me. I open my mouth to speak, but no words will come to me. I'm too overwhelmed, and for the first time in my life I can't think of one thing to say.

He lifts his hand slowly as if to ask permission to touch my face. When I don't move away, he gently caresses my face with the tips of his fingers. "Fuck those rich, uppity assholes. Don't let them get to you. From what I've seen, you're too good for them."

I shake my head and sniff. "No I'm not. They're right. I don't belong—not anymore." With that admission I cry harder. "I've got to go."

I turn and run again—away from Tyler. Away from everything that is my life. It's time for me to start living in my new reality, and letting go of a life that no longer belongs to me.

AVERY

I don't want to be packing right now, but I don't really have a choice in the matter. I haven't been to any classes since the party two weeks ago and I'm too far behind now to even attempt to go back and finish spring semester. I withdrew from all my classes this morning and came to terms that moving out of the city to start a new life with my dad is the best thing for me right now. Since Dad filed bankruptcy, it's not the best time for me to be getting mixed up in loans that I know my family has no way of repaying.

Dad and I are both completely broke. All we have left is the money my granny has floated us, along with the one car we are allowed to keep.

The entire student body now knows that I'm the daughter of the CFO caught in a recent embezzlement scandal. Charity's been busy leading the charge to ruin my reputation with anyone who would listen—even my cousin, who also attends Ohio State, has heard the story. I'm sure by now all the people I know at school have had a good laugh at my expense.

Chance poked fun at me yesterday on social media, so I made the decision to delete all my accounts just so I won't have to see the evidence of being the laughingstock of all my so-called friends firsthand.

I would like to say that we're moving somewhere uberglamorous and exotic, so that we can put all this behind us and start a new life, but that's not the case. Where we're going is a total hole-in-the-wall town. I haven't been there in years. I'm moving to Wellston, Ohio. Jeez, just thinking of the name puts me to sleep. Why Wellston? Well, that's easy. That's where Granny lives, plus we have nowhere else to go. I'm *so* not looking forward to living with her. She's great and I love her dearly, but she smokes like a freakin' freight train, she cusses like a sailor, and I know she's going to be hell on wheels to live with. She's not the little-old-lady-that-bakes-cookies type, that's for sure, but she's kind enough to allow her soon-to-be-homeless son and granddaughter to move in with her. I have to learn to make the best of the situation because I honestly don't have any other options right now.

Dad loads the last of our things in the only car the court let us keep. Our Mercedes SUV is top-of-the-line. I pleaded with him to trade it in for something a little less flashy because it's going to stick out like a sore thumb where we are going, but Dad didn't want to walk into a car dealership and risk the embarrassment of being turned down due to his current credit predicament. We're lucky to have a car at all right now. Wellston isn't really known to be a wealthy area by any means. Matter of fact, it's a part of what's referred to as Appalachia—one of the poorest regions of the United States.

I know I'm going to hate it there. I'm already desperate to find a way back to Columbus as soon as I can. I even stooped as low as making plans with my cousin Stacy, whom I barely speak to. The plan is that I come back to Columbus and live with her and my aunt Donna, my mother's sister, once Dad gets back on his feet and I find a way to pay for my tuition. I want to finish my degree even though I'm still not sure what I want to do with my life. College seems like the only option for a decent future. I'll find a way to support myself, but I've always been told I need a college degree for that.

I don't like the idea of leaving Dad in his current state. He's been really depressed since everything's gone down and is overly emotional. I let out a big sigh as I stand there looking at my room for the last time. This is totally heartbreaking. I've lost everything—my house, the people I used to think were my friends, and even my mom because of all this. She can't take being poor. At least that's what she told us when she left two months ago after Dad broke the news about what was happening to him at his job. Even though Dad explained that he wasn't responsible for taking all the money that the investigators claimed was missing, he did confess to taking a little extra money off the top of his company's profits. Dad was the CFO, so he controlled the money, and when the VP of the company discovered what Dad had done, he took millions of dollars from the company and set it up so that my dad would take the fall for all the missing money. Once my dad's lawyers dug into everything, they were able to provide the court with a paper trail leading back to the VP, which is how my father escaped without any jail time.

Even with that, the damage to his career was done. He says no other company will even consider hiring him after everything that's happened.

My mother couldn't stomach the fact that she was married to a broke criminal, so she left, and hasn't contacted either me or Dad since.

Mom is now dating her plastic surgeon, according to her social media page.

Money is a crazy thing. When you have it, people stick to you like glue. When you hit rock bottom, people scamper away and never look back.

"You ready, kiddo?" Dad asks. "We have a long drive ahead of us."

"Yeah, I'm ready. I was just, you know . . ." I mumble.

"I know," he says softly, while giving my shoulder a reassuring squeeze. "I am so sorry about all of this, Avery."

I pat his hand that's resting on my shoulder. "I know, Dad. You don't have to keep apologizing to me."

"But I do. I feel like I've ruined your life."

"It's going to be okay, Dad. Me and you . . . we're a team."

He gives me a small smile. "I'm so lucky to be your dad. Thank you for not giving up on me."

I turn and wrap my arms around him. "I'll never give up."

It's taken a couple months for me to forgive him for everything, and a small part of me hoped that Mom would come around like I did, but I'm not holding my breath for that to happen anymore.

I put a lot of the blame for what's happening to our family on her. If she wasn't so greedy and hooked on impressing everyone, Dad probably wouldn't have felt compelled to take money that wasn't his to take in order to support Mom's lavish lifestyle.

Dad pulls back and frowns. "We should get going if we want to make it to Granny's before dark."

I nod. "Okay. I'll be right down."

As I watch Dad leave my room for the very last time, I think about how much has changed between us over the past couple of months.

Dad's always been the more nurturing parent, so I'm glad he's the one here to comfort me. He may not say much—less is more with him—but I know he's always there for me, which is why, right now, I need to be there for him. It's safe to say we won't be having an emotional therapy session during our drive to Granny's because we've already had enough talks about the situation. We've become really close the last couple of months. He used to be one of those stereotypical workaholic guys before he lost his CFO job at McMullen's Candy. I think he feels bad about not being around all those years, because lately he's been trying pretty hard to spend all his time with me. I think he feels responsible for Mom leaving, but he shouldn't take the blame for her walking out. That was her choice.

When I called Granny a couple months ago to report the news that Mom had left, she just laughed.

"That's total bullshit," Granny huffed with her twangy accent. "Your momma left because she's a gold digger. Plain and simple. I tried to tell Tuck that before he ran off with the little floozy, but no, he didn't listen. It was just a matter of time before this would happen. Hell, she probably ran around on your daddy long before he lost all his money."

I love that about Granny. She's the most real, in-your-face person I know. If you ever want an honest answer, just ask good old Granny. She'll tell you the truth, whether you really want to hear it or not. I spend more time on the phone with her, telling her all about my life, than anyone else. Of course, I always have to leave some stuff out. It's embarrassing to talk sex with your grandma. I'm definitely not going to tell Granny anything about that. The last thing I need is for her to get it in her head that I'm anything like my mother, willing to sleep with guys for money.

I pat the door frame of my room and sigh as I turn and leave it behind. Outside I spot Dad latching the trailer door shut on the U-Haul that's hooked up to a rigged hitch on the back of our expensive Mercedes. It looks completely ridiculous, but Dad says it is the only way to haul the little stuff we have left.

It's clear it's time to go. I look around and silently say my good-byes while sadness slithers through me.

I can't say I'm surprised that my Kappa Kappa Gamma sisters aren't here to see me off. I'd be kidding myself if I thought any of them were actually *that* close with me. Shit, they wouldn't have even let me in if I wasn't a legacy and Mom hadn't sent me to Lars—her personal trainer—to whip my ass into shape, after high school ended.

At the time, I hated her for it. She just took my hatred in stride, told me it was for my own good, and someday I would thank her for it.

I can't believe it, but she was right. Being pretty does have its advantages. I'm glad she made me over, got me to lose a ton of weight. I was getting pretty tired of getting pushed around by the in crowd during high school. I was their doormat. But things changed for me. After I dropped the braces and lost the weight, I started a new chapter in life—college. I'd never been on a date until I became a Gamma.

Sasha and Rosemary were the first Gammas to befriend me. I know they were only my friends out of their own selfish greed. It's easier to get attention from boys when you have pretty sidekicks, and Sasha made sure that I knew that's why she kept me around—because she said guys think I'm hot. She was my friend out of convenience, so I definitely won't miss her.

It's just sad knowing that I don't have one real friend in my life.

"Wake up, kiddo," Dad says, while shaking my shoulder a little. "We're almost there."

During a big yawn, I strain my eyes against the glaring sun that stings my sleepy eyeballs. As far as I can see, there's nothing but grass and trees. Everything is so damn green here and there's no sign of concrete anywhere.

It's been ages since I've been to visit Granny thanks to Mom, and I forgot how far away from everything she lives.

Every now and then, we pass a tiny little house or a trailer parked up on some hillside, and I can't help but notice how different this place is compared to my life in the city.

It reminds me of the setting for a random, cheesy horror flick. It makes me think that if we do break down, some deformed hillbilly will probably drag us into a dilapidated shack and eat us alive—just like what happened to those kids in *Wrong Turn*.

"Almost there," Dad mumbles as he turns down a narrow road.

The worried expression that he tries to hide every time he catches me looking at him hasn't changed much on the ride here. I think he's dreading living with Granny just as much as I am but he's trying to put on a good face. It's been a while since they talked, so I'm sure this is going to be completely awkward for him.

We drive under canopies of big leafy trees, and Dad looks up and smiles like he's reliving some pleasant childhood memory. I haven't seen him smile lately. Really smile, I mean. I can tell Mom leaving hurt more then he leads on, even if he doesn't talk about her much anymore. He turns the air conditioning off as he holds down the little switchy-ma-bob for the windows, allowing the spring air to wrap around us.

He inhales deeply through his nose. "I almost forgot what air smells like without the pollution of city life in it."

I follow his lead and suck in a huge breath. Huh, the air does feel crisper here. I never really got that old saying before, "Get out and get some fresh air," but now it's quite clear. I wonder if pollution really does make the air different in the city, or if I am just delusional from the drive.

We creep along the road and then leisurely turn onto a vaguely familiar gravel lane. I've forgotten just how far off the road Granny's house sits. The grass soars on each side of the car and I roll my window down and stick my hand out, allowing the weeds to tickle my hand as we drive along. This yard is really overgrown and looks nothing like I remember. Granny always took a lot of pride in her yard, but it's obvious that she needs a little help around here. I'm sure it's not so easy for her to take care of this place all by herself. It's been nearly five years since my papaw passed away, and even though Granny acts way younger than her sixty-five years, I still worry about how much time I have left with her.

The house comes into view through the thick trees that create a natural privacy fence around the front of the property, and it's a lot smaller than I remember. A little, white, two-story farmhouse with a wraparound porch stands before me—nothing fancy, just a modest home that appears warm and inviting. It's definitely a far cry from the lavish home we just left behind.

I can't believe this is my home now. What a culture shock. There's no way the three of us will be able to live in this small space together and not feel like we're crowding one another.

Dad pulls the SUV up close to the house, and it doesn't take long for Granny to come rushing out the screen door. She looks just like the picture of her I used to keep tacked to my bedroom mirror to remind me of what she looked like. Granny hasn't changed a bit. She's still short and cuddly, and wears her faded blue jeans that remind me of the eighties day we used to have back in school. The only thing that's changed is her hair, which has a little more gray in it.

Granny barrels toward the car, and there's no time to get out of the way, only time to prepare for one of her notorious bear hugs.

She doesn't even give me time to get out of the car before she whips open the door and wraps her arms around me.

If you ever get a hug from my Granny, be prepared to just about have the life squeezed out of you.

"Oh honey, look at how pretty you are. You were pretty before, but now . . . I bet your daddy has to beat them boys off with a big stick. I'm just so happy to see you," she coos in my ear as she hugs me tight.

I smile at her and squeeze her back. "I've missed you so much!"

Last time I saw Granny in person, I was about fifty pounds heavier and hadn't been put through Mom's beauty boot camp. Back then, I could never get a boy to look my way, but now . . . I've heard guys refer to me as hot. Things have changed so much since then.

Granny hasn't seen me since I overhauled my appearance. I should've taken it upon myself to come see her. I've been a little selfish over the past couple of years, but I want to change all that. I want to start caring more about others.

Dad opens his door and stretches on the other side of the car. Granny sees her opportunity to hug him and takes off after him. It's nice to see them embrace because they haven't seen each other in years.

Last time Dad was here, Mom was with him, and Granny didn't have a problem telling Dad right in front of my mom what she thought about his wife. Granny has never liked my mother, but Dad was so head over heels in love he didn't care what his mother thought. After that day, Dad and Granny never spoke. Granny refused to apologize for the way she felt about Mom and the fact that she called her a "gold-diggin' hussy" because she felt her opinion was justified.

It took a lot for Dad to call Granny and ask her if we could come live with her. That's how I knew our situation was dire because Dad swore he would never speak to his mother again after that. Of course no one would ever believe there was any bad blood between the two of them if they saw them now.

It's amazing how old grudges can disappear when people learn to let go. There's no awkwardness between them at all. Granny busies herself hugging and kissing him, while singing Dad's praises, neither of them mentioning the past to the other.

"I've missed you, baby," Granny coos as she pulls back and cups his face in her hands. "It's good to finally have you back."

I swear I see a little tinge of embarrassment on his face when his cheeks redden just a touch at the sweetness of her words.

"Well, come on, you two, dinner's a-waiting," Granny beckons as she turns and heads back toward the house.

And just like that, the falling-out between them is a thing of the past.

I follow Granny into the house because we haven't eaten since we left Columbus and I'm starving. A nice fresh salad followed by my standard pudding cup will totally hit the spot right now. I hope she has fat-free Italian dressing. Since I'm so weight conscious now, I tend to only eat salads for dinner so I can keep the figure I've worked so hard to get.

The house feels smaller inside than I remember, and everything is exactly the same as the last time when I was here. All the furniture is the same as when Dad was a kid. I wonder if I can con Granny into a little redecorating after I get her hooked on HGTV. This place can use some new life breathed into it.

The aroma of greasy food wafts in the air throughout the whole house, and it smells like absolute heaven. What I wouldn't give to not have to obsessively count calories. Dieting sucks, but I have to work extra hard to keep the weight off. I'm not one of those girls who is blessed with the ability to just eat whatever. My body is very curvy by nature, and if I don't watch my intake, I'll turn into one immense curve like before.

"Wash up and then sit down at the table for dinner," Granny instructs.

After I return from the bathroom, I find Dad and Granny sitting down at the square wooden table in the kitchen. My eyes dance over the spread that's lying out on the table—fried chicken, mashed potatoes, and all the works. This is bigger than most Thanksgiving meals I've had at home with Mom. I bite my lip, and wish like crazy I could indulge, but I need to behave and stick to a salad like normal. The only problem is there's no salad in sight.

Huh, maybe it's in the refrigerator. Granny knows that I'm on a salad-only dinner plan. I've complained to her enough about it on the phone. I can't believe that she's forgotten that's what I eat.

I sit down at the table next to Granny. "Hey Granny, did you get my dressing?"

"Nope, not yet. It's on my grocery list though," she says as she spoons a heaping helping of mashed potatoes on my plate. "I only go shopping every other week."

"Did you fix a salad for me, though?" I ask, puzzled.

She shakes her head, and my face muscles twitch, threatening to show my disappointment. I guess one little home-cooked meal won't kill me. I'll just run two extra miles tomorrow to make up for it.

AVERY

Life sleeping on a couch is rough. I miss my bed, but I miss the privacy of my room more.

A girl needs her own room. That's where we do our best meditating. When I got the grand tour last night and discovered my room is the couch, I wasn't happy, but I knew I had to be thankful that I wasn't sleeping on the streets. The silver lining in all this was when Dad told me that he already arranged with Granny to build an extra room onto the house for me. Seems as though Granny has a bit of money saved up and she wants me to have this. The only problem is that Dad says we don't have enough money to hire someone to build it, so he's going to do it himself.

I don't have much faith in my dad's handyman abilities. I've never even seen Dad as much as pick up a hammer. There's no way I can picture him constructing part of a building.

I'm almost positive that the room is going to be lopsided.

He reassured me that he knows a little about construction, and that my room will turn out just fine, but I'm still pretty worried about it. He even told me yesterday that we can use Granny's truck to go into town and start buying supplies.

It'll probably be the highlight of my day since there's not much else to do.

I hear some rustling in the kitchen and try to pretend I'm still sleeping when Granny starts yelling.

"Come on, rise and shine," she calls through the house. "Breakfast is ready. Get up. You don't want to sleep your life away."

That actually doesn't seem like such a bad way to go since she mentioned it.

I pull the blanket over my face and squeeze my eyes shut. This doesn't work though because Granny comes over, rips the cover down, and keeps up her relentless taunt about me getting up. I groan and then roll over and push myself up because it's obvious there's no sleeping late in this house.

We're having another huge meal this morning and it kills me to eat like this again. You'd think she would've learned not to make so much food since she's lived alone all these years, but she tells me that she's always made meals like this. Granny comes from a big family of eight brothers and sisters, and her mom was the one who taught her to cook, which was for a family of ten. I'm going to turn into a beached whale if I don't get back on my normal diet soon. I'll have to stop at a store somewhere so I can buy stuff that I'm used to eating.

The moment Granny's delicious home cooking hits my mouth, I close my eyes and fight back the urge to go into a full-on food orgasm in front of my father. It tastes that damn good. I know I'll regret it later, but right now I allow myself to indulge a little.

Dad and I eat while we listen to Granny rattle on about the local gossip. I don't know any of the people that she's talking about, so I zone out, staring at a scuff on the kitchen table and wondering if Dad put it there when he was a little kid.

"Avery? Avery? Did you hear anything I said?" Granny growls.

"Huh? About what?" I rush the words out.

"About your chore list."

"*Chores?*" My eyes widen. "You're giving me a chore list?"

"Well, you'll have some duties around here," Granny says sternly. "Everyone has to earn their keep."

I never did anything remotely close to a chore back in Columbus. We had a cleaning service that came in and did everything, but I guess that's not an option here, since we're poor and all now. I shift uneasily in my chair while Granny reads me a list of things I'm supposed to do every day.

One thing on the list turns my stomach and I have to protest.

"Whoa, clean stalls? That's like cleaning up their shit, right? I don't know a thing about horses," I complain.

"Well, it's time you learn about them," she lectures. "And watch the language. It's not right for a young lady to curse." Granny gives me a wink and I chuckle. Ha, it's fine for her to cuss all she wants, but I'm not even allowed to say shit? Not fair and she knows it.

After I help with the dishes, I make my way outside for a bit of fresh air.

I plop down on the front porch steps and stare into the green nothingness that surrounds the house. I guess I should be grateful for Granny's chore list. At least it will give me something to do.

I stare down at my nails. I'm in desperate need of a manicure, but that's just one more thing that I can no longer have.

"*There's no money for frivolous things,*" Dad told me on the way down here. "*We'll have to just make do, and learn to live within our meager means now.*"

"You ready?" my dad calls as he pushes open the screen door and steps out onto the porch with me.

"For what?" I ask, completely caught off guard because I'm still sulking over cleaning the horse stalls.

"To go to the lumberyard . . . remember? I'm going to start building your new room today."

"Oh. Right." I'd nearly forgotten about that.

I push myself up and Dad wraps an arm around my shoulders. "I know things are tough right now, but things can only go up from here." He kisses me on the top of my head. "Come on, kiddo."

I follow Dad out to Granny's truck and then jump inside the cab with him. He twists the key in the ignition and the engine roars to life. Granny doesn't drive it much, but it still seems to be in perfectly good condition.

Dad pats the dash of the truck. "This was your grandpa's pride and joy. He bought it new in eighty-eight, and it was the first new vehicle that he'd ever owned. I remember the day he bought it. He was so proud, and he turned to me and told me that working hard is how you can afford to have nice things. I took that statement to heart."

Dad hasn't talked about his family in such a fond way in a long time, so it's nice to hear this story about him and his father. I want him to keep going, so I ask, "Is that what motivated you to go to college and move to the city?"

He puts the truck in drive and heads down the driveway. "It is. I always idolized the people I saw on television and all the nice things they had. I figured out early that if I wanted to have the kind of life I grew up dreaming about that I would have to be a successful business-man, so that's what I worked for."

This completely explains why Mom fell for Dad when they were in college. They were both money driven, and she could see that Dad had the determination to make something of himself. Mom knew that successful men typically marry intelligent, beautiful women, so she made it a point to get a degree in business, even though she never really planned on using it, or at least that's the way she put it to me when I was trying to decide on my own college major during my senior year of high school.

I turn my head and stare out the window. It's hard for me to think about my mother because every time I do, I just get angry.

These roads feel like they take forever, and there are so many curves. Between Granny's beat-up old truck and the fact Dad thinks we're in the backwoods Indy 500, my stomach turns with a little carsickness. I feel like sticking my head out the window like a dog to lap up some fresh air to help ease my turning stomach. Instead, I close my eyes, and take a deep breath, while trying to get my mind off my mother.

Relief floods me when we slow down and drive onto the straight city streets. I sit up to inspect my new town. There's nothing but a few fast-food joints and a local Walmart. Not only does there not seem to be anything to do in this town, but it appears that the job outlook around here isn't very good either, considering there are not a lot of businesses.

I suddenly feel the urge to take back every mean thing I ever said about Columbus. Compared to Wellston, Columbus is a huge city with lots to do, even if most of the people I know there right now are complete assholes. I miss being there already.

Dad turns sharply into what appears to be the local lumber store parking lot. The building is old and dilapidated. If we were back home this place would have plywood nailed tightly over the windows to keep the crackheads out. However, here it's an open business, proudly serving all the people of Wellston, according to the sign.

"Wow. A little rough, isn't it?" I ask.

"Come on, Ave, it'll be fine. Give this place a chance. The people here may not have much, but they're friendly." Dad smiles.

I sigh as I push open the heavy truck door and follow Dad. I can't bring myself to be argumentative with him. When he worked all the time, he barely knew I was alive. It was easy then to snap at him with bitchy comments, because I truly thought he was a jerk. Now I know different. He stressed a lot over his job and now that that's no longer in the way, we've really had the chance to reconnect and mend things between us.

I drag my feet aimlessly behind Dad through the lumber store. I'm not familiar with any of the things they sell, so none of it holds my interest, plus it smells weird in here. It has an aroma of musty wood and oil. My nose wrinkles up at every whiff I get.

I nearly jump for joy when he says it's time to go check out because I'm completely out of my element in here. I've never been in a lumber store before, but it's not high on my list of places to visit again anytime soon.

We walk outside away from the wretched stench of the store. I'm glad for a clean gulp of air. The more I get of this clear country air, the more I crave it. Normally I'm the biggest inside person you'd ever meet, but here it's different. I like sitting outside every chance I get. There's a peacefulness in being surrounded by nothing but country.

"Wait here," Dad says while thrusting the lumber receipt into my hands. "I'll go pull the truck up to the loading area."

Standing there like an idiot, I watch him walk away. I hate being in public alone. It makes me feel like a total loser with no friends. I slide on my oversize Dolce & Gabbana sunglasses, and gaze at my nails to appear preoccupied. People clamor in and out of the store. This place appears to be the central hub for all things construction.

"You waiting to get loaded?" a male voice asks.

"What?" I question. The word *loaded* to me only means two things: being rich, which I'm definitely not anymore, or getting high. No way do I need drugs. My life is screwed up enough without adding that to the mix.

I turn to confront my would-be dope dealer and my mouth drops open the moment my eyes land on the guy who asked the question. "Tyler?"

His eyes widen as soon as I mention his name. "Avery? I barely recognize you with those big glasses. It's great to see you."

"What are you doing here?" I ask, still amazed to see a familiar face.

My eyes trail up and down his body unabashedly because I know he won't be able to tell that I'm checking out that sexy tattooed body of his while I have these shades on. I'm usually not attracted to the country-boy type, but Tyler looks absolutely tasty in his faded blue jeans and his tight T-shirt and baseball cap.

He smiles and it lights up his entire face, even causing his blue eyes to twinkle a bit. "I work here."

"*Here*? I thought you lived in Columbus?" I ask, confused by why he works two hours away from where I met him.

"No. I've lived here my whole life. I only stay in Columbus on the weekend. My band's lead singer, Jimmy, has a place there. It's more convenient to do that since we play most of our gigs on the weekends. It's too far for me to travel back and forth, especially since most of our gigs don't end until late."

I nod. "That makes sense. I just didn't expect to ever see you again."

His top teeth graze over his lower lip. "Likewise. But I'm glad you're here."

We stand there in silence, and I know he probably wants to mention the last time he saw me—the night I ran out of the frat house crying—but he doesn't ask and I don't bring it up. That was one of the most embarrassing nights of my life and I don't look forward to rehashing the details of it anytime soon.

Finally, after some awkward silence, he clears his throat. "Can I see your receipt?"

"Oh, sorry." I hand him the small piece of paper.

He takes the receipt as his mouth quirks into a little grin. "So I take it you know someone down here since you're buying all this lumber."

"Yeah, my grandmother doesn't live too far from here, and my dad and I are staying with her for a while."

His eyes flick to mine, and I'm sure he's a bit confused as to why I'm living down here after he's seen my old house, but I don't give him any further details, so he just simply says, "I bet I know your grandmother, seeing as how this is a pretty small town."

"Her name is Geneva Jenson."

Tyler's gaze shifts upward like he's going through some file in his brain, searching for Granny's name, and then whips his eyes back to me. "She's out on Dark Hollow Road, right?"

My eyebrows shoot up. "Yeah. That's her."

He grins. "There aren't many people around here that I don't know."

I laugh a little. "Obviously."

Tyler opens his mouth to say something, but quickly closes it. He's looking at me like there's more he wants to say but is holding back. After a long moment, he jumps back into business mode. "Pull your vehicle to the side over there and I'll get your supplies loaded up."

"Okay. I'll let my dad know when he brings the truck around."

Tyler nods and then hurries off into the building.

Dad pulls the truck up and I jump into the passenger seat so I can show him where he needs to park. I watch closely in the side mirror as Dad helps Tyler load my room supplies in the bed of the rusty pickup. Tyler's muscles flex beneath the tattooed skin on his forearms as he stacks the wood we just bought carefully into the bed of the truck.

I can hear their voices inside the truck, but I can't make out exactly what they are saying because of the muffled sound. Dad is chatty though and he's laughing. He talks to Tyler nonstop the whole time they work. Tyler nods and smiles politely at him every now and then, but also seems to be answering a lot of questions. It's probably a job requirement to be friendly here.

"Okay, see you tomorrow," Dad tells Tyler as he opens the driver's side door.

Tomorrow? I examine Dad thoroughly through my sunglasses for a clue as to what he means, but I get nothing. Sometimes Dad can be very hard to read.

"Why can't we get whatever it is we need while we're here? Why do we have to come back tomorrow?"

"We're not coming back here. Tyler's going to help me with your room," he answers.

My gaze shifts over to Tyler, who is standing just outside my door filling out some paperwork. He catches me staring at him and a huge grin spreads across his face as he waves good-bye to me as Dad pulls the truck away.

Looks like I'll be seeing a lot more of Tyler around this town.

TYLER

Damn. It's hot as hell out here. I wipe beads of sweat from my face. This job sucks so much. I can't complain to anyone about it, though. People tell me I'm lucky to have a job in this shit town in the first place. Half of the people in Wellston live on welfare, so to most, I'm doing pretty well for myself.

The problem with this job is that it's so monotonous. I've got too much time to think, and that leads me into trouble. So many brilliant plans trickle from my brain during my shifts at Jones's Lumber. This is where I finally decided I'm ditching this town for somewhere better the day I get enough money saved up to rent an apartment in the city. There's no life for me here. This town has no jobs, no place to get my music career off the ground, and the girl situation . . . let's just say that no one turns my head here. Yep, this place sucks for a young, single guy like me.

"Yo, Tyler!" Blake yells over the walkie-talkie. "Customer needs loading out front."

That's my cue to hustle my ass up front so I can sweat my balls off. Loading customer vehicles is grueling. The customers usually just stand there, watching me break my back as I load their shit in their cars or trucks. Some people are so lazy they won't even put their own tailgate down to help me out.

I stride out of the loading dock, and nearly pass out. My God, she's gorgeous. She is by far the hottest girl I've ever seen in this town. This girl's body is smokin'. She's rocking a pair of Daisy Duke shorts, a navy-blue tank top, and some oversize sunglasses. I think I even see a hint of a black bra. Damn, she's sexy. She looks like a movie star with her sexy brunette hair and sense of style. I can't tear my eyes away from her. I would give anything to have a girl like that.

"Tyler, did you copy that?" Blake squawks again on the radio.

"Yeah, yeah, I got it," I answer him back.

"You need any help?" The walkie-talkie buzzes.

"No, no, I got this one."

No way do I want Blake out here with her. If I'm ever going to have a shot with this girl, he can't be around. Blake is our town's unofficial badass and my best friend. He rides a motorcycle and owns a Mustang, and all the girls think he's "so cute." No. I don't need him here to mess up my game.

After a couple more seconds of just watching her, I decide I need to say something, so I don't look like a total perv. I notice she has a receipt in her hand and my mind jerks back to the reason I'm out here. I almost forgot she's the customer I came to see.

"You waiting to get loaded?" I ask.

It's then that it strikes me that she looks just like the girl I've been dreaming about for the past couple of weeks.

"What?" She's clearly startled, and then the expression on her face morphs into surprise. "Tyler?"

My heart does a couple thumps as I realize that this is my real-life dream girl standing in front of me again. There're so many things I want to say to her, but I hold myself back and allow her to lead the conversation. Things don't go exactly as I would like, and there's a bit of weird awkwardness between us. I can tell that she's embarrassed about the way I saw her last time, but I want her to know that she can trust me, so I don't push the issue.

I stand there grinning like an idiot. Usually, I can think of a thousand witty things to say, but standing in front of her, I've got nothing. My brain is a big glob of Jell-O inside my skull. I'll admit, I'm intimidated a bit by her hotness.

Damn it. Still nothing.

So I do the only thing that makes sense, and turn the conversation back to the reason we're both standing out here awkwardly by asking for her receipt.

After I instruct her on where to have the vehicle loaded, I turn back toward the building, completely embarrassed. I hurry inside to get her order together, all the while scolding myself for not being a little more suave.

Stupid. Stupid. *Stupid.*

Man, I'm such an idiot. Why can't I talk around her? That was probably my one and only shot, and I royally screwed it up.

When I come back outside with the forklift that's stacked with their order, her father is standing at the rear of the truck with the tailgate already down. Her dad's help with the work surprises me. He's a really nice dude. He rambles on about how he grew up in this town, and how he and his daughter are here to stay for a while. In addition, he tells me that's why they're at Jones's Lumber. To get supplies to build Avery a room onto the house. *Avery.* I love the way her name feels on my lips.

"So, do you think you could help me out?" Avery's dad asks. "I can't pay you much, but I could really use the help."

"Oh, yeah. No problem." I don't even bother telling him that I would be willing to work for free because it will give me ample access to Avery—that would just make me sound like too much of a creeper.

"Great, I plan on starting it tomorrow. Will that work for you?" he asks.

"Sounds good," I answer. Definitely sounds like a plan.

He starts walking toward the front of the truck where Avery is waiting. "Okay, see you tomorrow," her dad calls.

Avery's lips draw in a tight line. She's confused about the tomorrow thing, probably.

She shoots me a look, and I waggle my eyebrows up and down, while my grin widens. I usually don't have to work this hard to get girls. This one is going to take a lot of effort, but I'm willing to put in the work.

AVERY

Day one of the room addition extravaganza kicks off rather slowly. Every time I get a minute break from Granny's slave labor, I check on their progress. I think Dad and Tyler spent the first half of the day figuring out how the laser and tape measure work because it took them nearly all morning to simply use a can of orange spray paint to mark lines on the ground. My suspicions are now confirmed, my room's going to be lopsided. I'll probably be in there sleeping one night and get crushed to death because the roof decides to collapse on me. So I wouldn't be surprised if "GIRL KILLED BY HOUSE" is in the paper someday. Maybe I don't want the new room after all.

Finally, with all my chores done, I earn a little free time. It's a rather warm day for May, and an itch for a little vitamin D hits me. After I change into a pair of shorts and a tank top, I plop down on a rickety plastic lounge chair. If I can't afford to pay for my tan anymore, I'll get it the old-fashioned way. I lay back and close my eyes, and wish I'd charged my iPod last night. The sun burns down on my skin after a couple minutes. It feels soothing. I get to pretend for a little while that things are exactly as they were. We still live in Columbus, and I'm at the pool in my backyard.

I enjoy the dream until a shadow blocks out my sun.

"That'll cause cancer, you know," Tyler says.

The sound of Tyler's deep voice causes me to nearly jump out of my chair. My eyes snap open to find Tyler standing there with a tool pouch around his waist. He's wearing an old rock band T-shirt with the sleeves cut off, allowing a full display of those delicious arms of his. He unbuckles the tools from around his waist and my eyes dart to his crotch for a moment. My face instantly flushes to a deep red when I realize he's caught me checking out his package.

I need to say something—anything to take my mind off the fact that I've just really embarrassed myself.

"I know the UV rays are bad for you, but I just want to look good," I finally answer. "And tan fat looks better than pasty white fat." Or so I read in one of my weekly girl-how-to magazines.

He laughs. "Well, if that's the case, you don't have a thing to worry about. Your body looks perfect to me."

I try to hide my smile so he doesn't think flattery will get him anywhere, but I can't hide it long. I bite my lower lip to keep from full-on grinning like an idiot.

Tyler just stands there staring as if he's studying me, and after a moment he shakes his head as if waking himself up out of a daze. "Sorry," he says, "I nearly forgot what I came over here for. Your Dad needs some more supplies. He didn't have any cash, so he wanted you to come with me to sign the debit card receipt."

The thought of being alone with Tyler again causes goose bumps to erupt all over my skin and I pray he doesn't notice.

"All right, but I have got to go put on some clothes first," I say.

"You don't have to. I mean . . . um . . . I think you look fine," he replies, looking a little red in the face.

"*Fine?*" I mock, raising an eyebrow after the compliment he just gave me moments ago.

I like making him squirm a little. That's the price he has to pay for ogling my boobs. I know he's checking me out. He is part of the male species, after all, and with a set like mine, they're hard for any guy to ignore.

I peer at him through my shades and wait for his recovery.

"Come on, you know what I meant," he says.

I laugh as I get up and sashay into the house to grab a different shirt, knowing that he's watching as I walk away. Even when I'm inside, I still feel his eyes on me.

"So where are we going?" I ask in a singsong voice as we get into Tyler's rusted pickup truck.

"Well, we've got to get some string to lay out the foundation," he answers. "The lines we painted today give a good visual, but now we need to measure how high up we need to lay the blocks for the footer. The string is a guide to make sure we come up high enough and stay level. It doesn't really matter what kind we use or where we get it."

"Ah." I say it like I understand what he's talking about, but in reality I don't have the first clue as to what he's talking about. Maybe he and Dad know a little more about construction than I've been giving them credit for.

"Anywhere you want to stop?" he adds.

I shrug, nowhere comes to mind. I'd only been to town once with Dad, but I would bet money they don't have any stores that I like to frequent. Besides, even if there were a place I'd like to shop, it's not like I have any extra money to spend.

Money wasn't an issue before, not when Dad still had his job. I miss those days. You never realize the privileges that you have until you suddenly lose them.

I'm completely lost in thought about our money plight when Tyler cranks up some strange music. It takes me a couple of seconds to place it, but then I realize it's country music—a kind of music that I never listen to. This shocks me a bit, seeing as how Tyler has more of the rocker bad-boy vibe going, not to mention he plays in a pop-rock cover band.

"Do you mind if I change the station?" I ask and then reach over and spin the dial vigorously, searching for anything with a tech beat.

"Hey, hey, hey . . . what are you doing?" Tyler harps, while swatting my hand away from the buttons.

"I don't really *do* country," I answer with a grimace, hoping that I haven't offended him too much.

"What? Who doesn't *do* country?" he says with a laugh, pushing the button to start replaying his CD. "This is the best song ever."

I lift both of my eyebrows. "This song?"

"Yes. The meaning. God, just listen to it. It gets you right here." He points to the spot on his chest that's directly over his heart. "This is real music." He steals a glance at me. "Just give it a try. It's awesome."

It's hard not to want to love the song after listening to the conviction in his voice. He's so passionate about it. How can I not give it a chance like he's asked, even if it's not necessarily the music that I typically enjoy listening to?

It's a song about a father losing his son. The song is about love and how even when you've gotten over losing someone, you never really move on—that you still hold that person close in your heart every minute of every day.

I don't consider myself an overly emotional person, but this song could make even the hardest man in the world shed a tear or two.

I bat away a couple tears that have fallen from my eyes, and Tyler reaches over and takes my hand in his and gives it a little squeeze. "Told ya. Right in the heart. Even tough ones like yours."

I roll my eyes. "I'm not that tough."

Tyler glances over at me and winks. "Sure you're not, crowbar."

We both laugh, remembering the first night we met, but it only momentarily distracts me from the fact that Tyler is now holding my hand. His palm is a little rough and I assume that's from working in the lumberyard. I've never had a guy reach over and take my hand like this before while driving and I have to admit that I like it a lot. The butterflies in my stomach are going crazy right now.

Tyler pulls into the parking lot of Walmart, parks, and then runs around to my side of the truck to open the door for me. Instantly he reconnects our hands and leads me inside.

After we get everything that Dad and Tyler need, we head back to Granny's place. For the ride home Tyler turns the radio station to a pop music channel and we jam to songs we both know all the way. Tyler and I sing most of the choruses together, but I have to admit, his voice puts mine to shame. He doesn't complain about my singing though. Well, not much, anyway. He does laugh and shake his head a few times when I try to go all Alicia Keys on him. Tyler is extra cute when he smiles, and I even notice when he full-on laughs, two little dimples love to make an appearance. Dimples are so sexy on a guy and they send my hormones into overdrive.

We hop out of the truck once we're parked at Granny's, and I instantly catch a whiff of her country cooking. I don't know how many more of these meals I can take, considering I've probably gained five pounds since I've been here. I've got to get stuff to make my salads before I die from heart failure from all the grease she cooks with.

Dad's waiting on the porch for us. He calls for me and Tyler to come in and get some lunch. Granny does most of the talking while we eat—most of the time she questions Tyler about his family. Appears Granny loves to know all about the town gossip. Suddenly, I don't feel special because she listened to all my problems for all those years while we spent hours on the phone every week. I listen as Tyler tells her about his mother.

"She's doing better," he says. "The first six months were rough on her after Dad died, but I think she's doing a lot better now."

I feel a little twinge of sadness for him. My heart goes out to him instantly knowing that he's recently lost his father.

"That's good to hear. I've been real worried about her," Granny replies. "When my Earl passed, I realized that you never really get over losing the love of your life. The first six months is the hardest." Granny reaches over and pats Tyler's hand. "I'm here if either of you need anything."

"Thank you," Tyler says and then gives her a small smile.

After lunch, Dad asks me to come out to the construction area with him because he wants to show me a few things. Tyler trails close behind us to assist Dad with the explanation of their plans for this addition onto the house.

They both try their hardest to get me to envision my new room, but for the life of me, I can't picture it. I don't have a very vivid imagination. So unless something is concrete in front of me, forget it. I won't see it. My main concern, here, is how long it'll be until it's done because at this rate, it'll be a while. Right now, there are only a few post holes dug in the ground and a bunch of tools lying everywhere. I'm still not convinced this is a very good idea.

"Dad, this seems like a lot of work. I really don't mind just sleeping on the couch." I attempt to give him an out if he feels like he's in over his head with this project, but Dad doesn't take it.

"Don't be silly, Avery. Granny really wants you to have this room. It will probably take a few weeks. There's only so much Tyler and I can get done in a day, but don't worry. It's going to get done," Dad answers.

"I'll be here as much as I can, but I work at least five days a week at the lumberyard. Hopefully, we'll get it finished before the summer is over," Tyler adds.

"I really appreciate all your help on the place, Tyler. It will be nice to have my own space while I'm here," I admit.

He smiles. "I'll do all that I can to see that we get it done."

"Okay, I'm going to take some of these tools into the barn to keep them out of the weather. Avery, honey, will you help Tyler carry all of his tools to his truck?" Dad asks.

"Sure thing."

I turn to Tyler once Dad is gone and ask him which tools are his so I can start picking up. Tyler points out a couple hammers and a few other weird-looking metal objects, so I grab them and carry them toward his truck.

I sling Tyler's tools into the bed of his truck. I never pictured Tyler as being a handyman type when I met him a couple weeks ago, let alone a guy that owned a bunch of tools.

"Jeez, if you wanted me to stay, all you had to do was ask. You don't have to throw my tools around like that and try to break my truck. I mean, I know those hammers are no crowbar, but I still worry about the safety of my truck when you are near it with any kind of metal," Tyler says in a mocking tone.

"Ha, ha. Very funny," I tell him.

"Good thing these old tools are tough. They can take a beating from the likes of you, I think." He smiles and those dang dimples come out again, making me a little weak in the knees. I expect another wise-crack from him any second while he continues to put away his tools, but every time he sees me glance at him, all I get is another smile.

"Okay, look. I know that you're obsessed with me, so if I ask you out—show you a little attention—will you stop staring at me all the time?" He chuckles.

My mouth drops open. Someone's awfully full of themselves. I'm not even sure how to answer that. I know he's kidding around with me, but is it that obvious that I really am staring at him all the time?

"Come out with me tonight?" he asks.

"You want to go out with me?" I question while wearing a teasing smile.

"Well, usually I think it's only fitting we go out on a real date seeing as we've already been out to Walmart and all. I don't take girls there until at least the second or third date . . . but you're special, and since our little trip together today was sort of our date number three, we can just pretend tonight will be date number four." He grins.

"Date four, huh? What's in store for girls on date number four?" I ask, playing along.

"You'll have to say yes first. Then you'll find out."

I absolutely love the way Tyler is so playful. I can really see myself falling for him, so I need to remind myself to take things slow with him and figure out if he's really the nice guy that he seems to be. All I ever seem to attract are jerks, but Tyler seems so different from all the other guys I dated back on campus. He's nice and seems to genuinely care about more than just himself. He was there for me when my friends bailed, and he was the one who came out to check on me at the frat party, and both times he didn't know me at all. Today when he took my hand, I felt a connection with him, and I really want to see where this will lead. It will crush me if he isn't as genuine as he appears to be. But, I'll never know unless I give him a real shot.

"Why not?" I smile.

"Yeah?" he says, sounding a little hopeful.

"Yeah."

"Great. I'll come back and pick you up about seven thirty."

"Sounds perfect."

I'm so excited to see what Tyler has in store for a real date, and I know it's going to be hard to control myself around him tonight. I find him ridiculously attractive, and that could be a very dangerous thing because I'm not quite ready to go through heartbreak again so soon. If it turns out Tyler is only interested in me for sex, I might just give up on the entire male species.

AVERY

The sun is still perched in the sky when Tyler comes to pick me up. I glance down at the clock on my cell phone. It's seven thirty on the dot. The guy is punctual, I'll give him that.

"So where are we off too?" I ask, while sliding on my trademark D&G shades as he fires up the truck.

"Well, I figure since it's date number four, I'd take you to get something to eat over at the local burger place, and then we could just hang out at a local spot I know," Tyler answers.

"I haven't been out to eat in a while and I've been dying for a good salad." God knows I need to start eating them again. I know I've only been at Granny's a few days, but I can already feel the fat stockpiling in my body. Man, where's Lars when you need him? He would die if he knew I've been stuffing my face with fried food and skipping my run every day. I keep telling myself I'll run some extra miles to work off all the greasy deliciousness, but I never have. I'm not lazy, *exactly*, I just don't want to run down some back country road all by myself. I've seen all the movies. I know what happens when girls go off by themselves in small wooded towns like this.

"You know, you look great, Avery. You don't need to eat *just* a salad for me. I like a girl with a little meat on her bones," Tyler says.

Obviously, he's never met fat Avery. Guys don't really mean it when they say those kinds of things. Guys will make comments like that to me now that I'm pretty and thin, but when I was a little chunky, they wouldn't have given me the time of day. Hypocrites, that's what all guys are. They have no idea how hard women have to work to look good.

"Right," I say. "I suppose you would've asked me out if I weighed about fifty pounds more."

"Of course I would've," he replies like it's the most obvious thing in the world.

That's a little hard for me to believe, seeing as how I wasn't asked out one time while I was in high school. He'll say anything to get in my pants, just like all the guys back home. Guys from my high school would try to feed me lines when they saw me after graduation like how they always noticed me, and how they wanted to talk to me, but they were just too shy. Give me a break. They weren't too shy to ask me out after I started wearing skirts and showing off a little more skin. Guys must think we're total idiots.

We ride in silence the rest of the way to the burger joint as I silently wish that I'm wrong about Tyler. That he's not superficial and is really the nice guy that he portrays himself to be.

On the other side of town, Tyler turns into the parking lot of the drive-in restaurant. It reminds me of those places in the old fifties movies where the teenagers would hang out on the weekends. It's like Sonic, but only it's old school. The sign even says EST. 1952, so clearly this place has withstood the test of time.

We park under the car canopy and Tyler rolls his window down, since the menu is on his side. Tyler presses a red button that alerts the restaurant staff that we're here. Tyler rattles a few items off the menu to me while we wait for someone to serve us.

It's hard to picture Mom and Dad at a place like this. I wonder if my dad ever brought Mom here when they were dating in college. As long as I can remember, they've never really gotten along. They fought constantly, and Mom just never seemed happy.

Granny said she never cared for Mom. She once told me on the phone about the day Dad brought Mom home to meet her for the very first time. Granny said she knew right then and there that Mom would break Dad's heart.

Granny must be psychic, because that's exactly what happened.

"So, what do you want?" Tyler questions as he looks over the menu through his open window.

"A house salad, with fat-free Italian, please," I say.

Tyler turns and points his gaze directly at me. "I thought we already went over this. You don't have—"

I hold up my hand to cut him off. "It's for me, okay? I like to keep track of what I eat, is all."

"Avery," he says my name so softly that it makes my stomach flip. "This is a burger place . . . get a burger, please," he pleads. "Besides, I don't think this is exactly the best place to get a salad. No one comes here for those, so the stuff would probably be all rotten."

Eww. Gross. That thought never crossed my mind before, but now that he's brought it up, my stomach churns.

"Okay, fine. But I expect to see you bright and early to help me run a couple extra miles to work it off," I say in a teasing tone.

He looks at me and smiles. "Deal."

The waitress finally comes out wearing a pin-striped apron over her white oxford and takes our order. When she's gone, Tyler and I make small talk about the city of Wellston and what a typical Friday night is like around here for single people like us. From what I gather from Tyler, there's nothing to do, which is why he spends most of his weekends in Columbus.

The next thing I know, our waitress returns with our food. She takes care to clip the tray onto the side of Tyler's truck before she scurries off. After he divvies up everything, we sit in the cab of his truck with greasy burgers and fries on our laps. Not the most glamorous of first official dates, even though he claims this is date number four, but it's kind of perfect. There's no stress to try and impress him. Tyler seems content just being in the truck with me.

I practically inhale my burger, fries, and shake. It's been a long time since I allowed myself to eat anything like this and I forgot how wonderfully sinful a mouthful of fast food tastes. It's like heaven in a wrapper. I keep having to mentally remind myself why I must limit myself with this kind of food. I don't want to become Avery Gravy again.

I shudder at those words. I haven't thought of that name for a couple years now and I've done my best to keep that painful memory bottled up. Brad Rutherford ever so graciously gave that name to me in the sixth grade when I got upset because I couldn't have a second helping of mashed potatoes and gravy during a class field trip. Everyone laughed, of course, when Brad started taunting me. I cried, but no one noticed. I was invisible—no one ever took the time to see me as a person who had feelings. All people ever focused on was the outside. Kids at that age never care how the fat girl feels.

I shake my head to clear my mind and decide that I'm going to enjoy this meal and to hell with the dietary consequences.

Every time I sneak a glance in Tyler's direction, he's watching me. That makes me feel a little self-conscious.

What is he staring at?

Doesn't he know that we girls like to chow down without someone watching our every move?

"Told you that you'd like the burger." He smiles, clearly pleased that I'm enjoying the food.

I nod, without saying a word. I can't open my mouth to say anything even if I want to. I'm struggling to just breathe around the meaty goodness. We finish our respective meals and Tyler heads out for the next part of mysterious date number four.

We drive around town, and he gives me the lowdown on what's hot here in sticksville. Not much, but I can't say that that shocks me. When we drove through town yesterday, there was a whole lot of nothing.

Just as I think Tyler is about to take me back home and call our date officially over, he turns down a road leading out of town in the opposite direction of Granny's place. The scenery here is pretty. Everything is overly green and looks like a landscape from a painting. The beauty of country living could really grow on me. No one is in a hurry, and everything seems simple compared to the hustle and bustle of my old city life.

The truck slows to a creep and Tyler moves the indicator, signaling we are turning into the woods. It's a road, I think. The only reason I'm guessing that is because the path is beaten down by what appears to be tire tracks.

"Uh, where are we going?" I ask nervously.

I have every right to feel skittish. It's nearly dark and he's dragging me into a deep, dark forest. Not a place I want to be, exactly.

"You'll see," he says.

We bounce along the path, until we reach a little clearing in the woods. I can make out a stream flowing into what appears to be a freshwater pool. There're even some old rickety lawn chairs strewn around. Tyler turns the truck around and backs up near the water.

"It's so beautiful out here," I say, and honestly mean it.

"I think so too. It's one of my most favorite places to hang out."

He cuts the engine, jumps out, and rushes around the front of the truck to my door. He offers his hand to help me out of the truck.

How sweet and suave.

Tyler's warm hand holds mine tightly as he leads me to the back of his truck. I don't miss the small, circular motions his thumb makes against my skin. It feels nice, and soothing, having him this close to me.

Tyler flips the tailgate down, and I immediately notice a guitar case in the bed.

"You play that thing pretty well," I say, remembering back when he played at the party with his band.

He grins. "Yeah, I'm all right, but drums are really my thing. Come on, I'll help you up," he says as he pats the shiny black tailgate.

I nod, and that's all the permission he needs. He puts his hands on my waist, and we stand there, face-to-face. For a minute, I think he's going to try to kiss me, but instead he tightens his grip and hoists me up.

He joins me in one swift motion. This boy is smooth, I'll give him that.

"So, where are we exactly?" I ask.

"This is a place we locals like to call the Sucker Hole."

I furrow my brow. "Why do you call it that?"

He shrugs. "Because they say only suckers swim in a freshwater pond in the middle of the woods. Lots of thirsty snakes in these woods, you know."

I laugh and tell him there's no way that I'll be getting in *that* water anytime soon.

So, now I can relax because he's cool with not trying to get me to go skinny-dipping with him, which was what I initially thought he might've brought me out here for. I stare up at the tall trees, and the way the sun is barely visible behind them makes me a little nervous about being here so late.

"It's going to be dark soon. Don't you think we ought to get out of here?"

"Nothing is going to get you, Avery. You're more likely to get attacked in Columbus than out here. You won't be hearing *Deliverance* music anytime soon." He laughs as he glances toward his guitar. "Believe it or not, there're some good people here. You just have to give them a chance, and besides, I'll protect you."

Okay, *now* I feel stupid. Maybe he's right. He's nice and pretty easy on the eyes. Especially with those dimples when he smiles.

Tyler opens his guitar case and pulls out a glossy blue instrument. Confidence exudes from him as he holds it. Very rock starish. I can picture him now making it into the big time, with a hoard of groupies swooning as soon as he takes the stage. Tyler is destined for fame. He's too good, from what I saw, not to be. He bites his lip as he strums the strings, moving his fingers along the frets to create a beautiful tune. When he opens his mouth to sing, his voice instantly soothes me. I've never heard this song before, but I love the rhythm of it and Tyler's voice is phenomenal.

I close my eyes and lean back, balancing my weight with my hands. This music is easy to get into, and before I'm ready, it stops, causing the forest around us to fall silent again.

I want to hear him sing more. He's unbelievably good. He could go on one of those singing competition shows and blow everyone else out of the water. He's that good.

"Play me something?" I ask with my most flirty smile.

I notice how attractive he is, sitting there during the twilight. There's something about a guy with a guitar that makes me giddy, and being in the back of this truck with Tyler at sunset while he serenades me is the most romantic situation I've ever been in.

I'm in awe as he starts moving his hands again rhythmically on the strings.

I don't know this tune either. Acoustic versions of songs are always hard for me to recognize. I watch his fingers as they glide sensually down the strings and can't help but notice how sexy it is.

When he opens his mouth and sings, my stomach tingles as a thousand butterflies flutter around inside it. His voice is even better like this—raw, with no distractions from his band pulling some of the attention away from just how great of a singer he is. A delighted smile creeps across my face. I'm genuinely impressed yet again by Tyler's talent. His sexability factor is skyrocketing at this very moment.

When the song ends, I clap. "That was amazing."

"Yeah?" He smiles. "I'm glad you're starting to come around to country music."

"That was country?" I ask, feeling a little dumb for not realizing. What can I say? I was a little distracted. "Huh, it didn't really sound country."

"Um, do you want me to play you a non-country song?" he asks, wearing a wry smile.

"Sure, go for it." I giggle.

He starts strumming a few riffs.

Before he starts singing though, he looks at me and says, "This one makes me think of you."

That shocks me a little. No guy has ever dedicated a song to me before, let alone sung one to me. It's romantic to know he thinks about me.

When he sings the first few bars, I know the song immediately: "I'll Be" by Edwin McCain. Sure, it's an old '90s song, but the light rock station back home plays it all the time. This is a deep song, one with meaning. I listen intently as he serenades me with a love song.

I look at him. I mean, *really* look at him, while he sings. He's so damn attractive. It's almost like I'm seeing him for the first time. His blue eyes dance in the evening light, and his lips look moist and very kissable. For a second, I picture attacking him in a fit of lust. Running my fingers through his blond hair, and pulling him down with me in the bed of the truck and . . .

Before I can finish my thought, the last chord vibrates. That's when I do it. I kiss him. I've never been the initiator before, but I can't help myself. I think I've surprised him just as much as I've surprised myself. His lips are soft and tentative. I can tell he's holding back and allowing me to take the lead. It's magic here in the bed of this pickup as we finally connect.

I pull away and stare into his eyes to gauge his reaction.

Tyler licks his lips, and a slow, seductive smile flirts across them. "Wow. Remind me to play that song every time we're alone together if that's the reaction I'm going to get."

I grin. "I bet you knew dedicating a song to me would score you a kiss."

"I was hopeful but never expected it to." He smiles as he leans in and caresses my cheek with his fingers and kisses me again.

It's nice, not overbearing or pushy, just sweet. I've never been with a guy who kisses so gently. Most of the time guys are too busy pawing me and ramming their tongues down my throat at this point to care about whether I'm into it or not.

This kiss, Tyler's kiss, seems different, softer maybe. Butterflies dance in my belly. Maybe he's into me for more than just sex. But, he *is* a guy, and guys usually only want one thing. Why else would he bring me out here? I want him to know that I'm into this moment—that I'm into him and am willing to go all the way if that's what he wants.

"So where do you want to do this?" I whisper.

"Wh . . . what?" he stutters.

"You know—do you have a blanket to put down or . . ." I trail off, waiting for him to fill in the rest of my sentence.

He pulls away from me and grimaces before turning to put his guitar in the case. He doesn't look at me, only concentrates on clasping his case shut. If I didn't know that he's a boy who had just been offered sex, I would say he looks pissed. That's not possible, right? What guy gets mad because you tell him you want to sleep with him?

He slides down off the tailgate of his truck, and lands with a soft thud into the semi-wet soil below. I'm puzzled. Am I being rejected? That never happens to me.

"Hey! Where are you going?" I ask loudly as he turns toward the cab of his truck.

He shakes his head. "I think this was a mistake. You're not the girl I thought you were."

Mistake? What the hell does that even mean? He looks disgusted, like the idea of sleeping with me offends him. What's his deal? I'm pretty. I'm hot. Guys practically line up to be with me back at school.

He's pissing me off. How dare he try to make me feel bad about myself? It took a lot for me to put myself out there like that, and his reaction crushes me.

"Whatever," I huff, jumping down to the ground, still feeling the sting of rejection.

Suddenly I can't wait to get out of here and away from him.

I take a couple big strides toward the passenger side of the cab, and Tyler, seeing that I'm ready to leave, heads toward the driver's side. Before I make it to the door, he grabs the side of his truck and looks at me from across the bed of the truck. "Hey, wait. Avery . . . look . . . I'm sorry. It's just . . ."

It's hard to make eye contact with him, knowing now that he finds me repulsive, but I need to hear him explain what it is about me that he dislikes so much. I stop in my tracks and meet his gaze from the other side of the bed.

"Just what?" I practically growl, fighting back the humiliating tears that sting my eyes. No one sees me cry anymore. I made a pact with myself after I saw the complete new me in the mirror the first time that I would never cry over a guy hurting my feelings *ever* again. So far, I've stuck to that promise, and I'm not about to let him have the satisfaction of knowing he's getting to me. "You don't like me, that's fine. I get it. I'm not the girl you thought."

It nearly kills me to say this out loud because it hurts way more than I thought it possibly could after only knowing him a few days.

Tyler doesn't reply. His hands grip the side of the truck, like he's holding on for dear life while he stares at the ground. I cross my arms while I wait for him to respond. It's like he's figuring out an explanation to let me down easy. I wish he would just come right out with it though. I need to know what he finds so repulsive about me, so I can fix it and never feel like this again.

"Shit," he mumbles. "I like you, Avery. You're funny, beautiful, and smart. And I can't believe someone like *you* would be into me like *that*. I want to have sex with you. Believe me, there's nothing more I would like to do than throw you down in the back of my truck and fuck you senseless, but I can't."

That makes no sense. This only confuses me even more.

"*Can't?* Do you have a girlfriend or something?" I ask. "I hope the answer is no because you know how I feel about cheaters. This time I won't chicken out when I get my hands on a crowbar when it comes to your truck."

He shakes his head. "No. No girlfriend."

I furrow my brow. "Then what's the problem? I like you and I thought you liked me too after the way you sang that song to me. I don't understand."

"I know it doesn't make sense, and I'm not really sure how to explain it. Get in the truck," he says, not responding to my question, merely dancing around it.

"Why? Why should I?" I snip and it comes out sounding all kinds of bratty, but I'm hurt and it's in my tone.

Tyler's eyes soften. "Please, Avery. There's something I want to show you."

I stand there unmoving for a few moments wondering what on earth he would need to show me that would explain the reason he doesn't want to sleep with me. I should say no, because he's already said enough to hurt me, but my curiosity wins out and I hop into the cab, ready to solve this mystery.

AVERY

We bounce down the rocky path away from the Sucker Hole toward the road. Neither of us says anything else to the other. I don't have the faintest clue what Tyler wants to show me, but now I'm curious as hell. Besides, I don't have any other choice but to go with him. Being stranded out in these woods wouldn't exactly be the ideal situation.

The tires chirp against the blacktop as they make contact with the main road. He's in a big hurry now for some reason. I hope he doesn't think my offer still stands, because he totally ruined *that* moment.

Tyler's eyes stay focused on the road in front of him as his lips twist. He appears to be worried and lost in deep thought and that scares me a bit. Whatever he wants to show me must be something that's upsetting and I'm not sure how much more I can handle tonight.

Then it hits me. I bet he forgot to bring condoms. That's why he looks upset and said that we couldn't have sex. Now for his comment about not being the kind of girl he thought. He probably didn't think I'd go for him so quickly and that's really sweet, but he should've known better. He's hot and I wouldn't be out on this date if I weren't into him.

All of this makes sense now, and it won't surprise me if he pulls into the next convenience store we see to buy condoms.

About the time I start feeling secure with my internal rationalizations, he makes a left into Pleasant Hill Cemetery.

This doesn't exactly look like a gas station.

My eyebrow arches and I bite my bottom lip. "Um . . . what are we doing *here*?"

"I'm going to try to explain to you why I couldn't—can't . . . you know," he says.

Right. How is taking me to a creepy cemetery close to dusk going to explain anything—other than maybe he's a freak? I hate being isolated in the country, let alone this place, and to top it all off, it's going to be dark soon. It's so scary. What in the hell does he need to show me in here?

He parks the truck under a huge maple tree and cuts the engine. He licks his lips and lets out a huge sigh before he turns toward me. "Come on. I want you to meet my dad," he says.

Wait. What? His dad is dead, from what I had gathered the other night when Granny mentioned his family at dinner. It's kind of morbid he brought me out here on a date. This guy clearly has issues and it makes me begin to worry about my safety.

"Um . . ." I say hesitantly.

He holds his hands up, palms out. "It's okay, Avery. I know this is weird, but I want to tell you about him, so you'll understand me, and why I . . . can't have sex with you no matter how much I like you."

He's obviously still dealing with his dad's death or whatever, so I'll go along. Maybe it'll help with closure.

"Okay."

I follow his lead as he gets out of the truck. He stops beside me and reaches his hand out to me. I grip it tight, because honestly I'm a big chickenshit when it comes to spooky places. Haunted houses even scare the crap out of me. I know it's all fake and everyone's an actor, but the last time I went I got so freaked out I almost peed my pants, so it's nice that he wants to stay close to me out here.

We walk down the hillside and stop at a grave that looks much fresher than the others. No wonder he's still weirded out about his dad. It doesn't look like he's been dead all that long. I glance at the tombstone that reflects in the twilight. It says he died a little over six months ago.

I can't imagine what it's like to lose someone you love so much. Sure, my mom's not around anymore, but she's still alive and I can call her whenever I want—if I wanted to, that is. I mean, I know she's a bitch and that she sucks royally for what she did to Dad, but she's not out of my life for forever like Tyler's dad is out of his.

"I'm sorry about your dad," I say and give his hand a little squeeze.

He doesn't really say anything, just stares at the big slate rock at the end of the newly sprouted grass. It must be hard, knowing your dad's under all that dirt—not being able to touch him, hug him, or hear his voice.

I wipe a tear from my eye and choke back the lump in my throat. What would I do if that was *my* dad? I would probably break down, crawl into a hole somewhere and completely shut down, not wanting to live anymore without him.

Tyler drapes his arm around my shoulders and rubs my arm and I find his gesture sweet. What kind of guy comforts a girl who's crying in front of *his dad's* gravesite when she should be the one comforting him? I don't know what's wrong with me. I'm not sure why I feel this way about a man I've never even met, but I think it has a lot to do with the fact that I can empathize with what Tyler's going through.

"I don't mean to freak you out or upset you by bringing you here, but I felt like it was something that I needed to do so you'd understand," he says, then pauses, taking in a shaky breath, and continues, "My dad was everything to me. My hero. The man I looked up to and wanted to model my life after. He and Mom always seemed so happy, and that's all I ever wanted in life—to find the kind of happiness they had. It wasn't until Dad got diagnosed with cancer that he began talking to me seriously about my getting out of this town and making something of myself. On his deathbed—the last words he spoke I took to heart. He asked me to do something—something that may sound a little strange."

"What?" I whisper and my heart thumps hard in my chest. "What did he want you to do?"

"He told me to stop screwing my life up and to take things more serious. He told me to stop messing around with random girls, to just focus on my music dream, and to get the hell out of this town," he says with a sighing breath. "Dad always thought I would fall in love like he did and never leave this town because that's what happened to him. He and Mom got pregnant with me right after they got together, and getting a job to take care of his new family took precedence over going after a dream. He wanted to see me give my dream of doing music for a living a real shot before I settled down—to go after my dream before anything else got in the way so I wouldn't live a life of wondering what if, like he did."

"That sounds like pretty solid advice, if you ask me."

He smiles. "Yeah, it was. That's why I can't sleep with you. My plan is to get out of here as soon as I save up enough money. I'm going to Nashville. You know, give this music thing a try, and I don't plan on coming back here if that happens. It wouldn't be fair to start a relationship with you knowing that I'm going to be leaving."

I nod. "I can understand that. How close are you to saving enough money?"

"I've been on track to do exactly what Dad asked me to do, so I'm pretty close to making my goal."

My mind processes everything he's just said and it makes me curious about something else. "So you've not slept with anyone since you made that promise to your Dad?"

He shakes his head. "I've never had any girl cross my path who's tempted me—that is, until you. There's something about you that draws me in, and I can't stop myself from wanting to be around you. Ever since that night I gave you a ride home, you've been on my mind almost constantly. You are the most beautiful woman I've ever seen, and what's even more surprising, you've got a big heart. I've seen how easily you get hurt, and I think that's the sign of someone who is passionate and loves wholeheartedly. I find that unbelievably attractive, making you really hard to resist."

I bite my lip as I stare into his eyes. "You think I'm tempting?"

He takes my other hand in his and threads his fingers through mine while he faces me. "Let's just say now I totally get why Adam gave in to Eve and sinned. If he was attracted to her half as much as I am to you, there's no wonder that he risked God's wrath to be with her."

I don't even know how to respond to that. No guy has ever poured his heart out to me like this, and it's taking every inch of willpower that I possess to stop me from jumping his bones here and now.

I need to change the subject to get my mind off of how much my body craves his touch right now.

"So you want to be a country singer? Is that why you want to go to Nashville?" I smile. "You got the voice. And I bet you know all those twangy, 'I shot my dog' country songs."

He laughs. "Yeah, I know a few."

We stand there together, still holding on to one another while we gaze into each other's eyes.

So it's not that he finds me repulsive, because he said that he *does want* to sleep with me. He just made a pact to stay on the straight and narrow path until he gives his dream a try. I can respect that.

I've disappointed my dad in the past with my promiscuity. Dad actually cried when he walked in on Chance and me making out hot and heavy in my bedroom once. He wasn't even mad at me. He took all the blame. Which puzzled me, because don't parents worry about their nineteen-year-old daughters becoming sexually promiscuous? Dad told me he was sorry he wasn't around to teach me to value myself more than to throw myself at boys. Talk about a low blow. Nothing opens your eyes to your slut activities more than your Dad crying over it. I promised myself to slow it down, and I guess that's when Chance decided that Charity was a better, sluttier option to date.

I really shouldn't be sleeping around with random guys either. Maybe this staying celibate thing is a good idea. I wouldn't mind trying it out, but I know that I'll still crave closeness with a guy—I need human contact. Kind of like now, we're close and touching. And if I were to really do this celibacy thing, kissing would obviously be allowed. We just couldn't have sex. Perhaps, we could do this together, like a partnership, and I could get to know him without the pressure of having sex looming over me, and when he leaves I won't be completely devastated because we'll never be intimate. "I have a brilliant idea," I say and hope he doesn't think it's completely crazy. "Let's do this together."

He tilts his head. "Do what together?"

"You know . . . be a sexless couple together. We both need to stay away from sticky relationships with people in this town, because I don't see myself living here forever either. No one else will understand why we don't want to be tied to this place because of a relationship but us. While I'm here though, I don't want to be a complete hermit. I would still like to go out and enjoy the company of the other sex. So . . . I like you. You like me. We can, you know, be friends with limited benefits." I smile, seeing the brilliance in my own plan.

Tyler quirks one eyebrow. "You'd still date me, knowing that I won't have sex with you?"

I lift one shoulder in a noncommittal shrug. "There's no one in this town I'll like more than you."

"But you could," he challenges.

"That's not possible. No one will ever be able to serenade me like you can, or be there for me when I decide to break out a crowbar and do something stupid the way you do." That statement causes Tyler to chuckle, but I'm not done telling him what I like about him. "But besides all that, you're quite possibly the hottest man I've ever seen, so

I doubt you'll have any competition in that department either. So like I said, I'm sure."

He nods his head as he thinks about my offer. "As crazy as it sounds, I like your plan. Are we allowed to kiss, because I'll be honest, now that I've tasted your lips I don't think there's any way I won't want to do that again."

My heart does a double thump against my ribs. "That's definitely allowed."

He has no idea how bad I want to attack him right now. I don't think I'd be able to do this little plan if I wasn't able to kiss him, so I'm glad we're now on the same page. Hopefully this works out like I see it going down in my mind—me ending all of this with a good guy friend—a totally hot, kissable friend—and a relationship that's guaranteed not to break my heart.

AVERY

So after it's decided that we're going to give this new friendship thing a real shot, we decide to head home. I climb into the beat-up old Ford truck and wait for Tyler to crank the engine. It fires with a rumble that's starting to sound very familiar. I snuggle into my seat and click the seatbelt in place. I'm actually excited about this friends-with-limited-benefits plan. I'm tired of being hurt by men, so this arrangement works out great for me. For all intents and purposes it'll look like I have a totally caring and loving boyfriend, just no one will know our dirty little secret—that we're not really a couple. I'll appear to be a one-man kind of woman.

"We should have some rules," Tyler says while he drives me home.

"I totally agree. Setting boundaries is an excellent idea."

"We obviously go on dates, and hold hands, but we should limit everything else to keep from getting carried away."

I nod and smile. "That's sounds good. Anything else you planning to allow other than hand-holding and kissing?"

A mischievous grin lights up his face. "I don't think much else should be allowed, considering I find you insanely attractive. If we allow anything other than kissing, I can't be held responsible for my actions."

I laugh while I think about how nice his lips felt pressed up against mine, and a shiver rushes through me as I think about going any further than that. He has a good point. Anything other than a few simple kisses might cause us to veer off the plan. "Noted."

He guides the truck up the overgrown driveway leading to Granny's and then parks before he turns the key and the engine rumbles to a stop.

"So . . . should I walk you to your door?"

I laugh. It's cute seeing him ask permission to do anything. "That'd be okay."

He jumps out of the truck while wearing a huge smile. My eyes train on him as he walks briskly around the front and stops at my door. Tyler jiggles the handle until it opens. He takes my hand like a true gentleman and helps me hop out of the truck.

We walk hand in hand to Granny's front porch and then I turn to him as we stand there. "You're a really good actor."

"I'm not completely acting, Avery. I really do like you." He touches my nose with the tip of his finger. "Believe me, if I didn't have the fear that my dad is looking down on me from heaven and shaking his head in disappointment, I'd be all over you."

"You think he watches you from heaven?" I ask.

"I think he watches me all the time. Since he passed, I've felt his presence at different times."

"What do you mean?"

"There have been signs from Dad." Tyler holds up his hand. "I know that sounds completely insane because I never used to believe in that kind of thing either, but I've seen some things that have made me a believer."

"Like what?"

"Lots of things. Some small, a couple majorly mind-blowing. Like I can be driving alone and be thinking of Dad, and just talking out loud, pretending that he can hear me, and a song about a father's love will pop on the radio at that very moment. Or dreams that seem so real it's like he's right there with me. It's really hard to explain, and admitting it out loud to you makes it sound a lot crazier than it did in my mind, but it's like I know these are signs from him, pointing me in the right direction like he's my guardian angel. I want to make him proud of me."

"I have no doubt he is, and he's probably pretty proud of you for turning me down."

Tyler laughs. "I think you're right, and he knows how much of a struggle this is for me too."

It's crazy how when I was chunky Avery, a guy like Tyler would've laughed in my face if I'd thrown out an offer like I did earlier, which is why I immediately jumped to the conclusion that he didn't like me. I guess I should be glad at times like this that I have a mother who believes your looks and style are everything. She's the one responsible for starting me on a path to being healthier. To her being sexy is everything. I guess she was getting tired of me not gaining enough male attention so she pushed me to change.

"So," he says in a singsong voice and then clears his throat. "I guess this is goodnight."

"Yep," I say, popping my lip on the "p."

I've never been this anxious waiting on a guy to kiss me. Most don't give me the chance to build up any anticipation. Most take kisses from me if that's what they want. But Tyler is different than any other guy I've ever dated, and more than anything I want his kiss.

He grins, leans in, and gives me a little peck on the lips, but doesn't linger long enough to allow the fireworks that were building to explode.

I'm left unsatisfied because Tyler's holding back. If we are going to be *special friends*, I need a little more than *that* in the lip-locking department in order for this to work.

He begins to move away, but I'm not allowing him off the hook so easy.

I curl my fingers around Tyler's neck and pull his face back down to mine. "Oh, no. You're not done yet," I whisper, then plant my lips on his and wrap my arms around his neck.

His arms snake around my waist and he deepens our kiss. A throaty noise erupts from the back of Tyler's throat and he presses his toned body against mine. I can feel how much he wants me through the stiff material of his jeans. My pulse pounds in my ears as my panties grow wet.

Tyler pulls away and I let him this time because I feel satisfied with his last attempt.

He grins as he stares down at my face. I'm sure my cheeks are flushed as my mouth hangs open because I'd like nothing more than to continue this make-out session.

Tyler cradles my face in his hands before he leans in and kisses me lightly one last time. "Goodnight, Avery."

I flex my fingers in a slow wave as I watch him turn toward his truck. The moment he's out of sight, I press my fingers against my still-tingling lips. Stopping at kissing only is going to be a huge challenge for us both.

AVERY

As soon as I shut the door behind me, Dad shouts my name from his upstairs room. I take the stairs two at a time, surprised by my newfound energy. I still feel all fluttery inside. I'm just as excited about my relationship with Tyler as I would be if I were in a *committed* relationship. This is the first time a guy has ever made me feel this crazy after just one date.

"Yes, Dad?" I ask, nudging his door open a little more.

"You had a phone call while you were gone. I didn't mean to pry, but you forgot your phone here and I saw the caller ID when it was ringing. Your cousin Stacy called," he explains.

"Thanks. I'll give her a call back."

He nods with a worried expression. "Avery, I know it's a big adjustment for you here, and the easy way out of this situation would be to move in with your mom's family because they live in Columbus, but I hope you know things for you there won't be easy. Your aunt Donna isn't a fan of mine, and she's a lot like your mother. So I'm begging you to not make any arrangements to live with them. Please consider staying here with us—where you're loved unconditionally."

I'm sure all the recent visits with my cousin Stacy before we moved gave away that I was planning on moving back to Columbus with them as soon as I could. I don't like seeing Dad upset, so if he needs me to stay here with him a little longer then I will.

"Okay, Dad." That seems to satisfy him because he smiles.

"Thank you."

I head back down to the living room, feeling completely conflicted as to what I should do now. I do need to return the phone call and catch up with Stacy.

My fingers fly over the keypad as I search out Stacy's number from the speed dial. The phone rings twice and she picks up.

"Hey, Avery!" Stacy says with an excited tone in her voice.

"Hey," I respond. "What's going on? Dad said you called earlier, but I forgot my cell phone here while I was out."

We go through the motions of gossiping about people we both know from campus, and it seems that things are exactly the same as when I left. Stacy tells me that she saw on social media that Chance has dumped Charity, and has now moved on to yet another girl from my sorority. That guy is just begging for a girl who he wronged to chop off his penis.

Chance got off easy with me. I literally let him go without inflicting any damage in retaliation for him fooling around on me. Tyler is actually the one who saved that pretty car of Chance's. If Tyler hadn't interrupted me and made me question my actions, that car wouldn't have been shown any mercy.

"So, what's up with you?" Stacy quizzes. "You having any luck finding any yummy boys down there?"

I pause at the thought of filling her in about Tyler. She won't understand the relationship he and I have if I tell her the truth about us. Stacy is a total gossip and I know whatever I'm about to tell her will be blasted onto social media and then will trickle all around the Greek society. It would be nice to have her spread the word that I have moved on from

Chance and that I couldn't care less about him at this point. "Oh yeah, I'm actually already seeing someone," I admit.

"Well . . ." she pushes, "details."

I explain how Tyler is actually the guy who gave me a ride home when my sorority sisters left me stranded in the parking lot the night I went after Chance's car. She seems genuinely impressed by my tale of how we met again and he asked me out. I also tell her about the little lake he took me to.

"So how was the sex?" she asks, digging for dirt.

"We haven't . . . I mean, for God's sake, Stacy, I just met the guy!"

She laughs. "Calm down. I was only asking. I just assumed he probably got you in the back of that truck and then had his way with you."

The idea of Tyler taking me in the bed of his truck is a scenario that keeps playing over and over in my mind since earlier tonight. Stacy doesn't know how bad I wish that it had actually happened, but Tyler just isn't that kind of guy. He's the kind of guy who opens doors for ladies and rescues damsels in distress. He definitely isn't like Chance, who tried to get into my pants on the first night that we met.

"He's not like that. Tyler's a gentleman."

"I'm happy for you, Avery. I just hope he continues to be a good guy and isn't just putting on some act to get you in the sack."

"I really don't think he is. He feels too genuine for games."

I hope my gut is guiding me in the right direction this time. God knows I don't think I can handle two douche-bag guys back-to-back messing around with my emotions.

TYLER

Why did Dad have to throw a wrench in my game? Just when I thought I knew every girl in town, and that keeping my junk in my pants was going to be easy, Avery has to come along. Her sexy-as-hell body is making the no-sex-with-random-girls thing pretty damn tough. I'm already addicted to her. It all started when I spotted her in the parking lot, ready to fuck up her cheating boyfriend's car. Sure, it was a bit crazy, but I was amused that the hottest chick I'd ever seen was also a little bit of a badass. That made her hot, but when she decided she couldn't do it, I knew she also had a good heart, which made her even more appealing.

It was so hard not to jump her bones in the back of my truck when she put out the offer. The woman I have the hots for is all but begging for me to fuck her, and yet I couldn't bring myself to go against my promise to Dad. I mean, how many times does an opportunity like that present itself? Not many. But I know I did the right thing.

God, I can't believe I passed on that. What the hell is wrong with me? This is going to be so rough. I'm not sure if I can keep myself from breaking my promise to Dad if she keeps on looking at me with those sexy blue eyes like she wants to rip my clothes off.

This could be a good thing, though. I've never actually gotten to know a girl before without trying to get into her pants right away. The no-sex thing may take a lot of pressure off. After all, Avery knows the whole truth about *why* I can't sleep with her, and she seems cool with it. Maybe just having her around as arm candy will be enough to satisfy the obsession I have with her. She really is the prettiest girl around here, *and* she's funny, which is a definite plus. It's been a rough six months for me, and her ability to make me laugh is really awesome. I should really put some effort into getting to know Avery if this is going to work. She did invite me to go running with her in the morning. Damn it. I hate running, but if that's what she likes to do, I guess I should give it a try.

AVERY

Yawning, I close my eyes as I raise my arms over my head in an attempt to wake myself up. Sleeping on this couch sucks. Dad needs to hurry up and finish my room so I can sleep on a bed again. Sliding off the couch and stretching my arms over my head helps wake me up.

Ugh. My thighs are touching. I've gained about five pounds since I've been here because I haven't been on my strict diet and exercise plan. I really need to run.

So I decided to just get over my fear of running alone on these back roads, and force myself to get back into my regular routine. After dressing in my workout clothes, and throwing my hair into a messy ponytail, I skate out the front door.

A smile tickles my cheeks, and I try to fight it back, but I can't hide it. Tyler's outside my house, sitting on the tailgate of his truck.

He remembered.

I thought he was just feeding me a line yesterday, but now I realize he was very serious when he agreed to be my running partner.

Tyler's long legs are bare thanks to the shorts he's wearing, and I'm able to see the defined calves he's been hiding under those jeans. Like his arms, his legs bear multiple tattoos and it makes me wonder what other parts of his body are covered with ink.

He hops off the truck and joins me as I begin to stretch. I can't stop smiling like an idiot. He's putting in a lot of effort and I'm really impressed.

"Hey." He grins. "How many miles are we doing again?"

"Not sure yet. Just try and keep up, farm boy," I tease as I take off running down the driveway.

We run in sync, our feet pounding the pavement along the over-grown country road in perfect time. The morning sun beams down on my exposed skin, energizing me, encouraging me to push my body harder.

Digging my toes into the asphalt, picking up speed, I move a couple strides ahead of Tyler. Running is the one thing I'm good at.

With a grunt, he matches my pace. I laugh as I shoot him a side-ways glace and he wags his eyebrows. I love this playful side of him. He makes it so easy to just be with him.

"Is that all you got?" he taunts and takes off ahead of me.

I grit my teeth. No way I'll allow him to beat me. It takes me about two seconds to catch him and get back in his rhythm.

We finish our run, ending back at Granny's—well, technically it's my place too—both of us sweating profusely. It was the most exhilarat-ing run I'd had in a while, and I'm pretty sure the intense delight I'm feeling has more to do with the guy than the run itself. No man has ever invested so much time in getting to know me before, and I have to say, I like it.

I watch as Tyler hops up on his tailgate, drags a cooler to the end, and pops open the lid. After handing me a bottle of water, he gestures toward the swing that hangs from the two tallest walnut trees in the front yard.

We sit side by side, sipping ice-cold water in silence.

Silence. What a contrast to the chatty coverstation about our secret pact last night. I really don't know what to say, but I hope he isn't having second thoughts about the whole thing.

I can't stand the quiet. It was what my old house was filled with back in Columbus after Mom left us. It gives me too much time to ponder, so I have to end it.

"So . . . what are your plans for the rest of the day?" I ask.

"Well, first I have to work on your room with your dad, and then after that I wondered if you wanted to go out with me again? There's a party tonight," he replies.

"Party?" Finally something I'm used to. "I'm *so* game for a party."

Tyler grins. "Great. I can show you off. You'll be my arm candy."

I roll my eyes. "Okay, but only because you're my pretend boyfriend."

Tyler heads home for a shower after our run, and then returns a couple hours later dressed in blue jeans and another old rock band T-shirt.

I spend the rest of the morning watching Dad and Tyler work on my room. I have no clue what they're doing but I appreciate the view as I watch Tyler use a shovel to dig a couple trenches for the room's foundation. A sheen of sweat covers his skin as his muscles twist beneath taut skin. Just as I'm about to file Tyler's sexy forearms away in my memory vault, I hear the screen door snap back on its hinges.

"Avery?" Granny calls. "You need to get out there and get them horse stalls mucked."

I could pretend to ignore her, but I'm sure she'd just keep hollering, so I might as well get up and do as she asks. The quicker I get it done, the sooner I can come back here and ogle Tyler some more.

I grunt as I rise to my feet. "Dad, you do realize that cleaning horse crap is one of the most disgusting things on the planet, right?"

"I know it's gross, but Granny is old, and you'd really be helping her out if you could get it done," Dad says.

"You're right," I agree. "The thing is, Dad, I don't know anything about horses or how to take care of them. All I know about cleaning stalls is what I've seen on TV."

"Avery—"

"I'll help her, Mr. Jenson," Tyler interrupts. "That is if you don't mind that we take a break here for a bit."

Dad nods. "Go ahead. I'll finish cutting these last two-by-fours and then break for lunch."

"Sounds like a good plan," he tells my dad before turning toward me. "Lead the way."

We don't have to walk far. The two-story barn is only about four car lengths away from the house. The red paint that once covered the boards has peeled away over time, leaving the old wooden boards exposed. Dad says that when Grandpa bought this house, the barn was already in place and that it was customary to keep the barn fairly close because most families lived on the milk and eggs they farmed every day. It made it easier back in the day.

I lead Tyler to the front door and push it open. The barn smells just as bad as I expected and it takes everything in me to not plug my nose shut. There are six stalls, but only three of them have horses in them. I stare at the magnificent animals who stand so tall and regal as we walk past them.

Tyler pats the side of one of the stalls. "This old place is in pretty good shape. It's been well kept."

"This was my grandpa's man cave. Dad says he spent a lot of time in here fixing things and making sure the horses were well taken care of."

"It shows. This place has got to be at least one hundred years old," Tyler says. "You ready to get started?"

I shurg. "As ready as I'll ever be."

Tyler picks up a pitchfork and then hands it to me. "The first thing we have to do is move the horses out to pasture while we clean their stalls." He reaches in and pats the horse gently on the nose. "You have to show them that they can trust you. It's no different than any other relationship. Trust is key."

I like hearing this explanation from him, and it makes me think that he believes this in every facet of his life. I want to trust Tyler and so far I do. He's never done anything to make me think that he doesn't deserve my faith in him.

Tyler lifts the latch on the stall and leads the horse out of the barn like he's done it a million times before.

When he returns, he takes the pitchfork from me and says, "Now it's your turn."

"Me?" I ask hesitantly. "I don't know if I can."

Tyler smiles and takes my hand. "Don't be afraid. They won't hurt you, and I'll be right by your side."

His words are comforting and I suddenly feel a surge of bravery shoot through me, knowing that he'll be there to make sure things go right.

I lean the pitchfork against the wall and then make my way toward a stall that has a tall, tan horse with a dark brown mane. I uncurl my fingers and stretch my hand toward the horse and it neighs, causing me to jerk my hand back.

"It's okay," Tyler encourages. "Try again."

I swallow hard and then attempt again to touch the animal. This time it allows me to pat the smooth spot just above its nose.

A smile creeps over my face. "It's so soft. I haven't been in here since I was a little girl."

Tyler watches me openly as I overcome my fears. "Now you know there's absolutely nothing to be afraid of."

"Thank you for this—for helping me."

Tyler reaches up and pushes back a loose strand of my dark hair away from my face. "Anytime."

I bite my lip, loving the feel of his touch, and as I'm about to lean in and kiss him, Tyler clears his throat. "Let's knock these stalls out so we can break for lunch."

"Okay."

After we lead the other two horses out of the barn, Tyler shows me the best way to hold the pitchfork and scoop the straw and poop out of the barn. When he's statisifed that I can manage on my own, he picks up another pitchfork so we can finish in half the time.

Much to my surprise, Tyler is taking this work seriously. I find myself alone, in a stall, stabbing into a massive pile of straw and dung. A horse barn in warm weather is the worst thing I've ever smelled in my entire life, but I know it needs to be done. These animals deserve a clean place to stay.

"This is a lot harder than I thought. I'm only halfway finished and my arms are already burning," I admit.

Tyler's deep laugh rumbles in the next stall. "I won't say it's the most glamorous job in the world, but I'm sure there are worse ones. Like cleaning hog pens."

"I'll take your word on that one, because if it smells more awful than this, I don't want any part of it."

"This is pretty bad, though, but the faster we work, the sooner we can get out of here," he says.

We work quickly, trying to get eveything done, and just as the barn starts to smell a little better, my mind begins to drift to how things were for me just a few months ago. I wonder what my friends back home are doing tonight. My life here is a startling contrast to what it once was. It makes me curious as to what tonight is going to be like.

"This party tonight . . ." I trail off as I wonder out loud.

"Yeah?" he responds.

"What kind of party is it *exactly*?"

"I dunno, it's just a party. Are you asking me if we have a theme or something? Do we really need that to get together and drink beer?"

I laugh and then decide to tease him a little. "No. I wouldn't expect that much creativity from you country bumpkins."

"Hey now . . ." He chuckles.

"I'm just joking. But seriously, what should I wear to this unfestive drinking event?"

"Wear whatever you want. It's not like there's a dress code or anything."

"Well, can you at least tell me what the girls around here typically wear to a party? I don't want to be dressed wrong and stick out."

He walks into my stall and leans his shoulder against the rough wood wall and smiles, nearly stilling my breath. "Avery, I think you'll stand out no matter what you wear."

I give him my sexiest grin. He's flirting with me and this is an area I'm well schooled in. I want to keep this going. "Are you saying I'm noticeable?"

He takes a step toward me, pulls the pitchfork from my hands, and props it against the wall. His strong arms wrap around me, effectively crushing me against him. The heat from his body pulsates off of him, activating the delicious smell of his woodsy cologne. His blue eyes are fixed on me intently, only leaving my gaze for a second to stare at my lips, which causes me to lick them—inviting him to kiss me.

"You're *very* noticeable," he whispers before his lips meet mine.

My heart thuds in my ears as his tounge probes into my mouth, teasing me, and it makes me want more. My fingers lock into his thick hair as I hold him in place. This subtle gesture only excites him further. He swings me around and pushes my back against the scratchy wood. He breaks our kiss and then his lips trail down to my neck, leaving a fire in their wake. I run my fingers up and down his back. It feels good to feel so wanted by him. The way he can't seem to get enough of me even though I'm off-limits makes me feel powerful.

His hand slips under my shirt and I let out a soft moan before his mouth covers mine again. If we keep up this pace, things will eventually escalate beyond just making out, but I don't want to think about what that will mean for us. The need to be as close to him as I can rocks through me. I draw my right leg up and hitch it around his hip, this time causing him to groan as he grinds his pelvis into mine. Feeling him against me has me so turned on that I can barely see straight.

I reach down and find the button on his jeans. Before I can pop the button open, his fingers wrap around my wrist, like a restraint.

"Avery . . . you have to stop tempting me. I won't be able to keep telling you no."

"So don't say no," I whisper before I bite his bottom lip. "I want you so much."

I know I shouldn't encourage him to break his promise to his father, but I can't help myself.

"You know I can't."

I ignore his plea. My own greedy need overshadows any guilt I may feel for trying to seduce him. I move my hands back into his hair and press my body tight against his. His will seems to crumble as he grips my hips and presses me firmly into the wall. He glides his strong hand down my thigh and stops at the back side of my knee, guiding my leg back around his waist. Gripping the bottom of his shirt, I slip it up over his head and toss it across the top of the wood wall.

He follows my lead and slides my tank top up before throwing it on top of his. Tyler reaches behind me to release the hooks of my bra to allow access. He traces the white lace of my bra with the tip of his finger before he slides his hand underneath the cup of my bra. His hand on my bare breast sends shivers all through my body. I throw my head back and close my eyes, feeling victorious. I ache for Tyler to touch me all over, and just as I think I'm about to get what I want, I hear Granny calling my name.

"Oh, shit!" I hiss.

Freaking out at the thought of getting caught in this compromising position by my grandmother, I shove Tyler back, giving myself enough room to reach back and fasten my bra.

I toss his shirt to him. "Hurry up and put this back on," I say as I readjust my own clothes.

After pulling myself together, I turn to run out of the stall. Tyler grabs my hand and pulls me back to him and kisses me softly.

A broad smile dances across his lips. "I'll miss you."

I grin at my pretend boyfriend. "I'll see you later."

Before he can speak another word I turn on my heel and race out of the barn.

TYLER

I watch Avery run out of the barn and I realize my head is still spinning. I press my back against the wood and sigh. It's still warm from where Avery and I generated some major body heat. The images of what almost took place in this very spot dash behind my closed eyelids and that doesn't do a thing to get rid of my raging hard-on.

Knowing I promised my dad to behave, I can't help but wonder if he would give me a free pass for Avery. There's no way I can resist such an amazing woman forever. My old whoring ways won't hold back much longer if we keep this pace up, especially knowing she's obviously really into me and wants to have sex just as much as I do.

There are no words to describe how much I want her. Since I met her, she's the only thing I think about. No girl has ever had this effect on me. *Ever.* I've been with plenty of girls, but I've never met one who makes me feel all alive and tingly inside like I do when I'm with her.

My heart pounds erratically, like a jackrabbit loose in my chest and trying to pummel its way out, as my thoughts race. Whenever she touches me, my knees grow weak and I become somewhat tongue-tied. Usually, I'm the suave one—the say-all-the-right-things guy—while

Blake is my good-looking wingman. Together, we are the unstoppable panty-dropping duo.

But with Avery, it's different. Of course, I *want* her, but I think I may want more. No. I definitely want more. I want her to be *mine*, more than pretend. I want the real deal with her, and I know that it's wrong of me to ask that of her considering I don't plan on staying in this town, but I can't stop myself from wanting to take her.

The crazy thing is, I can tell by the way she kisses me back that she wants me too, and that only heightens my attraction to her.

I'm pretty sure we'd be having some pretty hot sex in this stall right now if her grandma hadn't interrupted.

The way Avery told me to stop saying no in her breathy voice still rings through my mind. I know Dad would be disappointed in me for saying this, but I think I won't be able to keep saying no to her willing body if this keeps up much longer.

I lean my head back against the wooden wall and shut my eyes. All of this built-up sexual frustration is clouding my judgment. My head is all kinds of mixed up. Avery knows that I won't be hanging around this town forever, so I don't think she would be upset if we sleep together and I don't put a ring on her finger, but I don't want to hurt her. I want us to still be friends once I decide to leave this place in search of my dream.

TYLER

I sit in the truck as Avery comes bounding down the front porch steps. She looks amazing in her short shorts and tank top, but then again she looks great in everything. Her dark hair is down tonight, with full-flowing, loose curls, and my fingers itch to get tangled up in them while I taste her lips again.

My cock jerks in my jeans at the very thought. Damn it. This is what happens every time I've thought about her since we were in the barn. I take a deep breath and focus on baseball to rid myself of the wicked fantasies going on in my brain. Tonight's going to be a true fucking test because I've already made up my mind that if she says yes to becoming my girl, I'm fucking her until she can't walk straight.

Avery opens the passenger door with a huge smile on her face. "Hey."

I love how happy she is to see me. "Hey, there, sexy girl. You look smokin' hot."

"Thanks." A blush creeps over her face as she pulls herself up into the cab of my truck.

Once she's settled in, I can't stop myself from leaning over and tasting her. The warmth of her hand on my face sends a little tingle through me as our lips connect. It's not an intense moment, but more of an I'm-glad-we're-together-and-I-missed-seeing-your-face kind of moment.

I turn my attention back to the wheel and throw the truck into drive. We bounce down the long gravel drive to the main road. Avery turns the radio to the pop station and begins singing along. It's funny how comfortable we are together. Maybe it's because we've been together so much lately—who knows—but I'm glad it's easy between us. She might just be "The One" that Dad worried would come along and make me want to give up my dream and settle down in this town.

"So this party . . . where exactly is it again?" Avery asks.

"It's at my buddy Blake's house. He's a chill dude. I think you'll like him."

"Hmm . . . maybe I'll like him more than you," she teases. "He might actually want to have sex with me."

The idea of Blake putting the moves on Avery makes my blood boil, and if I hadn't already staked a claim on her, that's exactly what would've happened. There's no way Blake could've resisted trying to get into Avery's pants. Thank God I met her first and have already threatened Blake with bodily harm if he tries to move in on her.

"Hey, now," I warn. "I never said I didn't want to have sex with you, just that we'd have to wait."

"Wait?" She raises one eyebrow. "I thought you took a vow of celibacy or something."

I laugh. "I never said that I wouldn't have sex for the rest of my life—only that I would wait until I got my career off the ground—and then I found the right girl who made me want to stop fucking around."

Avery grins. "Are you saying that I'm the right girl?"

I take my eyes off the road to steal a glance at her. "I think you might be."

"That's good to know." Her smile widens and she tucks a loose strand of hair behind her ear. "I think you're pretty special too."

That causes my heart to do a double thump in my ribs. "Guess there's only one thing left to do."

"What's that?"

"Make it official," I tell her. "Avery, I want you to be my girl-friend—for real this time. No fake shit. I'm talking the real deal, Tyler-and-Avery-sitting-in-a-tree kind of relationship while I'm still in town—even if I'm not here that long."

She unbuckles her seatbelt and slides across the bench seat of my truck to sit right next to me. I throw my arm around her shoulders and she leans in and kisses my cheek. She feels good sitting next to me. I don't think I ever want to let this girl go.

She leans her head against my shoulder. "You're sweet. I hope you're as nice as you seem."

I know she's probably worried I'll hurt her like that asshole ex-boyfriend she has, but I want her to know that I mean it. I think with a girl who's been hurt the way she has, actions speak louder than words, and I want nothing more than to prove that she can trust me with her heart.

I want to be honest and up-front with my intentions. While this thing between us might be short-lived, I want her to know that she means a lot to me, and my leaving has nothing to do with her. My plan to get out of this town has been in the works for a while, and I owe it to myself and my father to see it through.

We drive through the streets of Wellston and I pull up along the curb in front of Blake's house. It's an old two-story house with a bright blue paint job and a rickety front porch. It's not much. Working for barely above minimum wage at the lumberyard doesn't buy you a very lavish place to live—not even in this town where the cost of living is substantially lower than living in Columbus.

The screen door swings open and Blake comes stumbling out with a beer in his hand. He shields his eyes against the shine of the porch light and then waves us inside. "You comin' in or what, asshole?"

I shake my head and open the door. He's crazy, but I love the guy like a brother.

"Let me get the door for you," I tell Avery before I hop out and walk around the front of the truck. Once outside I whip my head in Blake's direction and flip him the finger. "What's your big hurry?"

A crooked grin lights up his face. "You know why I'm rushing you. Let's see her."

Blake's never been known for his patience, but you can't fault the guy for wanting to get a look at the girl I've been talking about nonstop for a week now, ever since I first met her in that movie theater parking lot.

I point my gaze squarely on him. "Remember. Hands off." I can't stop myself from giving him one last reminder. Unlike me, Blake has zero self-control.

Blake throws his hands up in surrender. "I know, man. No trying to bag your new piece. I got it."

I raise my eyebrows and point at him. "I mean it, Blake. Don't even—"

"Dude, you sound like a psycho. Chill." He laughs.

Maybe I do sound a bit crazy, but it's probably because the very thought of someone touching Avery sends me over the edge.

I pull on the door handle, and Blake tucks his beer between his arm and torso so he can rub his hands together like a little kid whose Christmas present is about to be revealed. I turn my attention back to Avery and give her a hand to help her out of the truck.

She smiles up at me as she steps onto the ground. "Is it weird that I find it sweet that you've kind of lost your mind when it comes to me? It's nice to feel so wanted."

A smile tugs at my lips. "It's no stranger than how being jealous is causing me to lose my shit, so I guess it's a good thing you find my possessiveness endearing."

"Holy shit!" Blake's words cut between us. "I'm sorry, bro, but I may have to say fuck guy code on this one and go for her anyway."

I wrap my arm around Avery and tuck her against my side. "Sorry, man. This one's taken."

Avery looks up at me and smiles and I know making a commitment to her was the right thing to do.

We slide up next to Blake on the porch and he grins. "Welcome to *mi* casa, where the liquor flows and clothing is optional. That especially goes for you, Avery."

I throw a quick jabbing punch into his shoulder. "Dick."

Blake laughs and holds his hand out to Avery. "I'm Blake and anything that you need, and I do mean *anything*, you let me know."

Avery shakes her head while she holds back a laugh, taking him in stride. "I'll keep that in mind."

"You do that. Come on. I need another beer." Blake turns and opens the screen door and we follow him inside. The house is crowded with all the usual faces that frequent Blake's little get-togethers, so all eyes fall on me as I escort a new one into their midst. "Everyone, meet the new girl, Avery." Blake turns toward my girl. "Avery, meet *everyone*. Now that that shit's out of the way, let's get fucked up!"

Everyone cheers and raises their drinks in the air, and suddenly the music gets cranked up and a lot of the girls jump up and dance.

Blake returns a couple moments later with a round of beers. "Let's drink to the new hot chick in town."

Avery laughs as she takes the drink. "I'll drink to that."

Blake downs his beer in one gulp and then belches loud enough to be heard over the music. "Have fun, you two. I've got something I have to take care of."

With that Blake files through the crowd, leaving Avery and me in the living room full of people I've known most of my life.

Bodies gyrate to the latest Top 40 pop song, in turn clogging up every spare inch in the living room. Avery and I weave in and out of the crowd and make our way into the kitchen, where the beer is kept. Blake and a few other guys I recognize from work are playing a very intense game of beer pong. If I had to guess, Blake's laid down some money on a bet. He always says money on the line makes the simplest things more interesting.

Blake tips his chin up when he notices us in the room. "You two want a piece of this action? You can play the winner of this game."

"I'm not sure." I'm hesitant, not sure if Avery would be willing to jump into the game, but the super-competitive side of me is dying to play.

Avery doesn't say anything, just sticks by my side as we watch the game unfold in front of us.

Avery kisses my cheek. "Want a beer?"

"Sure. Thanks," I say before she pulls free and heads toward the coolers that are full of beers, sitting in the middle of the kitchen floor.

Loud cheers from Blake's beer pong game jerk my attention back toward him just in time to see him high-five his partner. "Still the reigning champs. We've beat everyone in this fucking place."

I grab the ping-pong ball off the table and hold it up between my fingers. "Not everyone."

"Oh, shit," Blake crows. "Step on up. But you know how shit goes down in my house. You better break out some of that money I know you've been stashing away, because we're playing twenty bucks a game, and there's no fucking handicap because your partner's a chick."

"Sure you want to make that bet?" Avery flanks my side. "Because if you're challenging me and Tyler, I hope you're prepared to have your ass handed to you, Blake. I'm pretty damn good at this game."

Blake rubs his palms together. "Hell yeah! I love a hot chick who can talk shit. This is going to be fun."

"I hope he's good for the money." Avery smirks and then winks at me. "Because I'm about to take it from him."

I think I just fell in love. This is a new side to Avery—the little hustler—that I find pretty damn sexy.

We start the game, and she wasn't kidding about being good at this game. She sinks two balls in on her first two shots, forcing Blake to drink, and he instantly offers up a proposal for marriage, claiming she's the baddest chick he's ever met.

Avery and I stun everyone when we win the very first round. Blake quickly throws down a challenge of double or nothing, and we launch into another game.

Avery doesn't mess around. She's focused on the game, landing shot after shot as she digs her way to another victory. I'm sure being a student at Ohio State presented her with ample opportunity to play this game.

"Whoa. Whoa. Whoa. You can't bring some fucking beer pong ringer into my house and not give me a shot at a rematch," Blake whines as Avery and I bask in the glow of our back-to-back wins.

"Best two out of three," Avery challenges. "But if I give you this rematch, we've got to make it interesting. We've got to play for more than just money."

"Fair enough," he says. "Name your terms."

I hold back a laugh. The intensity over a game of beer pong is comical, but I have to admit seeing this determined, bossy side of Avery is a complete turn-on. It's nice to see her confident in herself, especially after the conversation we had earlier about how she worries about her appearance.

"Okay . . ." Avery trails off. "My dad and Tyler are working on an addition on my granny's house. If I win, you have to come over and help them out one day next week."

Blake takes a moment to ponder that and then says, "Deal. But if I win, you have to give me a kiss on the cheek."

That catches my attention and I can't hold my tongue on this. "No fucking way, Blake. We went over this shit already. Change your stipulation."

"Fine. Fine. If I win, then Avery has to come back over in the morning and clean the mess that is my house. It's always being trashed and could really use a woman's touch. The toilets, in particular, because those things are a fucking mess."

Avery shudders, and I'm sure the very thought of probably touching the barf- and shit-filled toilets in this place has disgusted her thoroughly. The bathrooms here are pretty fucking disgusting. I wouldn't take that bet.

"Deal," Avery agrees.

My eyebrows rise up in surprise. Damn, my girl has some balls.

Blake's face lights up. "All right! When you come over in the morning, you might want to stop and get a pair of rubber gloves and a bio-hazard suit, if you can find one. It's pretty rank in there."

"There will be no need," Avery assures him. "I don't plan on losing. Ever."

"We'll see about that," Blake taunts.

"Let's get this show on the road then." She takes a long pull from her beer and then grins wickedly. "Let's see what you got, Blake."

Avery and I work on the next game, but lose quickly to Blake. The way Blake explodes after his victory, you would think he'd just won the Super Bowl, but he shouldn't get so excited just yet. We've still got two more games to play.

The next game is just as intense, and when Avery sinks her ball into the last cup on the table, we all launch into a frenzy of shouts and cheers. It seems that most of the partygoers have now chosen to be spectators in our nail-biting event.

The last game has everyone on the edge of their seats. This one will make or break everything. Winner takes all.

As soon as we start the last game, Blake quickly sinks two balls into two separate cups for his team. Avery and I each take a cup and down the beer, and then take our turn shooting at the cups at the other end of the table. Avery surprises me and sinks two into the same cup, and I follow her up by sinking one of my own into a different cup. It doesn't take long before there are only two cups sitting on the table. One on our end and one on Blake's, and the first team to get a ping-pong ball into the cup wins. Blake's team misses their shot and Avery answers by putting the ball into the last cup at the end of the table and winning the game for us.

I scoop her in my arms as the room erupts in cheers. It's exhilarating to share this moment with her, and it hits me that I haven't had this much fun in a long, long time. Matter of fact, this might just be the best damn day of my life and it's all thanks to Avery. I don't ever remember being this happy.

I wish my dad were here to meet her. He would've loved her. She's beautiful and sassy but deep down I know she's got a sweet heart that needs to be reminded of how amazing she is.

Avery kisses my lips. I cradle her face in my hands and deepen our kiss, allowing our tongues to dance together. If we keep this up, we will end up sleeping together.

"Get a room!" Blake shouts.

Avery smiles as she still clings to me. "Glad you brought that up, Blake. We'll see you bright and early to help build my new bedroom."

Blake frowns. "Come on, Avery. Do you actually expect me to come work on your house for free?"

"Would you have really made me come over here and scrub your toilets?" she fires back.

Blake's lips twist, but he doesn't give an answer.

Avery nods and laughs. "Thought so. Like I said, see you bright and early tomorrow."

She turns to me with the biggest smile on her face and I instantly crush her against me. "You are such a badass."

"What makes you say that?"

I give her a crooked grin. "Not only did you just whip Blake's ass in beer pong, but I remember a certain scorned lady with a crowbar who was ready to bash a beautiful Camaro to smithereens."

She threads her fingers through mine. "But in my defense, he was a complete asshole."

I nod. "Any idiot who's dumb enough to cheat on you deserves far worse than a couple broken headlights."

Avery twists her lips. "Just remember that for future reference if you ever feel the need to stray."

I chuckle. "For sure. My old truck doesn't have full coverage, so you can bet I won't be pissing you off anytime soon."

"Good to know." She walks backward toward the living room and tugs my hand. "Come dance with me."

A song about finding a good girl to love blasts through the speakers and it strikes me to the core. It mimics a lot of what I'm feeling right now. The music rocks through me and the overwhelming urge to express to Avery some of the emotion I'm feeling rolls through me. I stare into Avery's eyes and put as much passion as I can into the lyrics as I sing them directly to her. I want her to know that this thing between us—whatever it is—means a lot to me.

My hands fit perfectly on her hips and we dance and dance until I can barely stay on my feet. When the next song begins to play, she leans into me and wraps her arms around my neck.

"I'm getting tired," she admits.

"We can go anytime you're ready—just say the word."

She looks up at me and grins. "Word."

This girl fits so perfectly into my world. I can see myself being happy with her for a very long time. She doesn't even know it yet, but I think I'm already beginning to fall for her.

AVERY

The next morning, I giggle to myself when I see Blake hop out of the passenger seat of Tyler's truck. I head straight for the guys from where I just finished cleaning the stalls as I dust my hands onto my blue jeans.

Tyler's face lights up as I embrace him in a warm hug. "Hey, beautiful."

I pull back and then give him a quick peck on the lips. "Hey."

It's funny how at ease I've become with Tyler so soon. I know it's really only been a week since he gave me a ride home that night, but I feel like I can trust him.

I flick my gaze over to Blake, who appears to be hungover beneath the dark sunglasses he's wearing. He pushes back his thick, dark hair as he surveys the area of the house where Tyler and Dad have begun working on the addition.

"I was wondering if you'd show," I say with a smirk.

Blake turns his attention to me and then shrugs. "A bet's a bet, and I never welch on a bet. You won, so here I am."

Tyler chuckles, and the sounds reverberates in his chest. "Doesn't mean he's excited about being here though. He bitched the entire way over here about being tired already, so I'm not sure how much help he's going to actually be."

"Fuck you, dude. Even with a hangover from hell, I'll still work circles around you," Blake snaps. "Get your tool belt and let's get this show on the road."

"Okay there, hard charger." Tyler's smile only grows wider, and I can tell this good-natured ribbing probably goes on between them all the time. Tyler kisses my forehead. "Got to get busy. I'll catch up with you later."

With that Tyler takes off toward the site and then motions for Blake to follow him.

The rest of the day I keep busy helping Granny around the house. She's been teaching me to cook. When I explained to her this morning that I'm worried about eating all the fried foods, she showed me how to make some pretty damn good dishes that are a lot lower in calorie content. As Granny puts it, no woman should live on salads alone.

Just as I'm about to set the food out on the kitchen table and call the guys in for lunch, my cell chirps, alerting me to a new message.

Tyler: *I can't stop thinking about you.*

I bite my lower lip and grin as I quickly tap out a reply, letting him know that he's a frequent face in my mind.

Avery: *Every time I close my eyes, I see your face.*

It sounds unbelievably corny and I can't believe I've just sent that message to a guy that I'm really beginning to like, but I meant what I typed. Tyler is really beginning to grow on me. For the last week, he's been my source of comfort. The person who's been there to help me when times are a little rough—the night he found me in the parking lot, the frat party embarrassment, and even being here in Wellston. Tyler has really helped me transition the last few days and realize that things aren't so bad here.

If I'm being honest, Tyler's actually the one thing that's made me really enjoy being here. He accepted me with no questions asked, and seems to really want to spend time with me.

It hurts my heart to know that the time we have together has an expiration date, but I understand why he needs to get out of this town. Wellston is no place to launch a music career. Tyler owes it to himself, his father, and more importantly, his music, to find out how far he can make it in the business.

"Let them boys know it's time to eat." Granny's voice interrupts my thoughts.

I nod as I fire another text to Tyler alerting him to come get his lunch.

A few minutes later, Dad comes in towing Tyler and Blake behind him. The guys take turns washing their hands and when it's Tyler's turn, he sets his phone down on the counter in front of Blake as he heads into the small bathroom that's off the kitchen.

Blake leans in and reads Tyler's phone screen and raises an eyebrow. "Who the hell is Crowbar?"

Both Tyler and I burst out laughing at the same time, and I find it endearing that he already has nicknamed me in his phone.

"That's Avery," Tyler replies while still chuckling. "You'll have to ask her about the nickname. It's all has to do with the way we first met."

Blake's eyes grow wide. "Oh, shit, bro. Avery is the crowbar-wielding chick? I didn't think Avery was the same girl as the crazy one that you told me about meeting. I thought they were two totally different people."

Tyler wraps his arm around my shoulders and tucks me close to his side. "Nope. She's one and the same."

"Avery, you never mentioned that you knew Tyler," Dad chimes in, overhearing our conversation in front of the bathroom door.

Obviously, I never wanted to have to explain to my dad about the time I nearly lost my mind and damaged Chance's car, but I can see the questions lingering in Dad's eyes as he waits for my answer.

"It's no big deal, really, Mr. Jenson. Avery and I met when I was playing music at one of the frat houses," Tyler says, stepping in and saving me the embarrassment of having to relive the Chance situation with Dad.

Dad tilts his head. "How does this explain the part where Avery had a crowbar?"

I lick my suddenly dry lips "I, um . . ."

"She found a crowbar to help me fix my friend's flat tire," Tyler jumps in and saves me yet again.

"That's not what you—" Tyler slaps Blake's chest openhanded, causing Blake to grunt. "Umph. What the hell, dude?"

"Let's eat." Tyler abruptly changes the subject and I'm grateful for it.

Tyler glances over at me from across the table as we make our way to take our seats and I mouth the words "Thank you" to him, letting him know that I appreciate him covering for me.

We all quickly eat our lunch. Blake never says a word during the entire meal because he seems so focused on shoveling down as much food as quick as he can. Granny only smiles as she notices this, and judging by the satisfied expression on her face, I would say she's loving that Blake can't seem to get enough of her cooking fast enough.

Tyler, on the other hand, keeps a light conversation going with Dad about the way the room is turning out and how their visions for the place are all coming together. It's nice to see Tyler get along with the one person who means a ton to me. Dad likes Tyler. He's never had anything but good words to say about Tyler and the type of man he is. He's earned Dad's respect—and mine.

I wish he weren't leaving because I can see myself really falling for Tyler if he were a permanent fixture in this town.

TYLER

My cell chirps again, and I laugh when I see Avery's latest message with a picture attachment.

Avery: *We miss you.*

Below it is a picture of her with one of the horses in the stalls.

Tyler: *I miss you too. Can't wait to see you tonight.*

It's amazing how easy our relationship has become over the two weeks since we made our no-sex pact. We've fallen into a routine. Through the week, when I work at the lumberyard, I don't see her much, so we stay connected via texting and simply talking on the phone into the wee hours of the morning. I've really gotten to know her by doing that.

She told me all about her mother, and how she left when the news broke about what happened at her father's job. We've talked about everything from our favorite colors to our favorite movies, but I can tell she's still holding back from me a bit about something in her past.

"Put your fucking phone down. We have to get this wood loaded up," Blake complains as he grabs a stack of two-by-fours and loads them onto the forklift. "I've never seen you this distractible before. Crowbar has you so sprung."

"*Distractible*? I don't think that's even a word." I roll my eyes and stuff my phone into my back pocket.

"You know what I meant, didn't you?" The wood bangs against the other boards when he lays down another stack. "So what's up with that? Are you in love or what, bro?"

I grab as many boards as I can carry and head for the forklift. "I don't know."

"How can you not know? Either you are, or you aren't. It's not that hard."

I sigh. "There's nothing I can compare the way I feel about her to. I've never been in love before, so how do I know if I am or not?"

A smirk crosses Blake's face. "My friend, you just answered the question. You're in love."

"What do you mean?" Curiosity runs through me. How in the hell does he think he can answer how I feel about Avery when I'm not even sure myself?

Blake leans against the forklift as I load the last of the wood on it. "When you didn't immediately deny that you were in love, that told me right away that you were in fact head over heels for the girl. If you didn't feel something for her—if she was just a simple piece of ass—your denial of being in love would've been immediate."

I open my mouth to argue that his logic is crazy, but quickly close it when I realize that I really don't know if I'm in love with her or not. She's all I think about. That much is clear, and I'm always anxious to see her, but does that mean I'm in love?

I mean, how does a person really know? It's not like there's a chart to go by to judge if what you're feeling is love.

Blake chuckles and then slaps me on the back. "Now I've got you thinkin'. See, you're in love. You just didn't realize it yet."

I stand there with my mouth agape as Blake climbs onto the forklift and heads out of the building so we can load the customer's truck. Since when did Blake become so damn observant and knowledgeable about matters of the heart?

The rest of the day flies by as I do nothing but think about the way I feel about Avery. How did I not know that what I was feeling was turning into more than an intense like? Granted, I've never felt like this, but I thought for sure I would know that I was falling in love before it was so obvious to everyone else.

Another texts pops up on my phone as I climb into my truck after work, and I smile when I see it's from Avery.

Avery: *Are we going to Blake's tonight?*

Seeing as how partying at Blake's on the weekend is really the only thing to do in this town, I type back a quick reply.

Tyler: *Yep. I'll pick you up at seven and we'll go eat before we head over. Sound okay?*

Avery: *Perfect.*

There's never drama with Avery, which is surprising considering how I met her. It seems like people at her sorority were not very good friends to her, so I don't believe Avery was able to be herself with those people. They didn't seem to accept her, unlike here. In this town, she just seems to fit in.

After going home and grabbing a quick shower and checking on Mom, I head over to Avery's place. When I pull up the long drive, I admire the work that Avery's dad, Blake, and I have accomplished in a few short weekends. We have the frame nearly complete. Soon, Avery will have a room, and I know it will make her extremely happy to stop sleeping on her grandma's couch.

Avery comes out of the door, and bounces down the front porch steps. She smiles at me as soon as she climbs up into my truck and shuts the door behind me. "Hi!"

I love that she's excited like this every time she sees me. It makes me feel pretty damn good because I'm always anxious to see her.

I lean over and press my lips to hers. She tastes like cherries—good enough to eat. I pull back. "You hungry?"

"Starving," she answers immediately.

We head over to the drive-in diner and then grab a quick bite to eat. The entire time we're sitting in my truck, I can't stop thinking about the conversation I had with Blake earlier. It is possible that I love this woman sitting beside me, but is it fair of me to tell her while knowing that it doesn't change the fact that I have plans to leave this town behind? It wouldn't be right for me to tell her that I love her and then walk away from her right after I say it. She'll believe that I never meant it, and I couldn't blame her for feeling that way because that's exactly how it will appear.

"You look lost in thought." Avery's voice pulls me away from the things going on inside my head. "Everything all right?"

For a moment I debate telling her exactly what's on my mind, but then decide against it. The best thing I can do is keep that fact bottled up inside me. It's the right thing to do.

I smile at Avery. "Everything is fine. I was just thinking about work." I know it's a lie, but I can't bring myself to tell her the truth. So I need to change the subject. "How was your day?"

Her eyes search my face, and I can tell that she's not satisfied with the quick change of subject. She places her hand on top of mine. "You know you can talk to me, right?"

"I do know." I nod, but I'm nowhere near ready to talk to her about this. I might come off as completely crazy for wrestling with these feelings after only knowing her for a little over three weeks. "Things will be fine."

As usual, Blake's party is in full swing by the time Avery and I arrive. I smile as a few of the girls at the party greet Avery with a smile.

It's nice to see that she's no longer the new girl, and locals are now befriending her.

The moment Blake spots us he heads over with three red plastic cups in his hands. He gives Avery and me each one and then shakes my hand, followed by a chest bump. "Nice to see you, man. I wasn't sure if you'd make it tonight after the conversation we had earlier. I thought you'd be holed up in some hotel—"

Avery furrows her brow, and I can tell she's suspicious, considering the way I was just acting when we were eating.

My heart hammers in my chest. This is not how I pictured letting Avery know that I'm developing a deep attachment to her. I don't need my buddy spilling the beans about my feelings, so I quickly interrupt him. "Whatever, dude. It's fine. We don't need to talk about work shit in mixed company."

"Okay . . ." Blake lifts one eyebrow and then drains the rest of his beer. "I've got to take a leak."

He disappears into the crowd of dancing bodies, leaving Avery and me alone in the middle of a crowded makeshift dance floor. Avery opens her mouth to no doubt ask about that exchange, so I spin her around in front of me while wearing a crooked smile on my face to distract her. I pull her flush against me and begin to rock in time to the beat of the music.

She places her free hand on the back of my neck and twirls a lock of my hair between her fingers. "Dancing? What else are you good at?"

I grin. "Lots of things."

"Like," she prods.

"If you keep being nice to me, maybe tonight I'll show you," I tease, knowing that I'm tiptoeing around dangerous territory.

She bites her bottom lip. "Then I better behave because I can't wait to see some more of your moves when we're alone."

My cock jerks to life in my jeans and just like that, this girl has me turned on like a fucking light switch. When she says things like that, it makes it so difficult for me to behave myself. It almost makes me want to say fuck everything and take her because I want her so damn much.

I press my forehead against hers and close my eyes as I groan. "That pretty mouth of yours is going to get you in trouble. I've been good and held back this long, but I don't know how much longer I can control myself if you keep talking to me like that. If you tempt me one more time, I'm liable to throw you over my shoulder and carry you out of here right now so I can have my way with you."

Avery grips a handful of my shirt. "I think I like the sound of that."

Those words out of her mouth unravel my last thread of willpower. My ability to resist my desire is nonexistent. I take her cup from her and hand both of our beers to some random blond girl next to us before I bend down and hoist Avery over my shoulder. I warned her.

Once she's up there, I smack her ass hard enough to make it sting a bit. "You're so getting it."

She giggles as I turn and head for the door.

I don't know if she realizes what she's done, but she's awakened a sexual beast who wants nothing more than to find his way into that sweet pussy of hers. She doesn't even know how bad she's about to get it.

AVERY

I can't stop giggling as Tyler carries me outside while everyone at the party cheers him on, shouting obscenities about fucking me good.

Men.

Tyler's large hands curve around my upper thigh as we make our way down the steps to his old beat-up truck sitting out front. He opens the passenger door and sets me down on the seat.

He's about to turn away, when I say something that stops him in his tracks. "All that and I don't even get a little preview of what I've just gotten myself into?"

Tyler turns and then threads his fingers into my hair. He pulls my face to his, effectively pinning me in place as he crushes his lips to mine. This kiss isn't gentle like all the others that we've shared. This one is filled with need and lust and it excites me. His tongue dances across my lips, begging for entrance. I open up, allowing him inside. The rhythmic movements of his tongue remind me a lot of when he played the drums back at that party on campus. Tyler's got natural rhythm. My legs spread apart and he grinds himself against me and I can feel how much he wants me.

He pulls back before I'm ready, leaving both of us panting while we stare into each other's eyes. I'm about to ask him why he stopped until he opens his mouth to speak again.

"We have to stop now or I won't be able to stop myself from taking you right here in this truck."

I take a quick glance up at the house and wonder if taking him up on that threat would be worth it. Seems everyone is back inside and they probably wouldn't notice.

Tyler shakes his head. "Don't even tempt me by thinking about it. I can guarantee that Blake is watching through one of the windows and I won't risk him seeing you. If anyone's going to see that beautiful body naked, it's going to be me, and only me."

His possessive words make me shiver. I've never had a guy act like that with me before, and if I'm being honest, it's a total turn-on. I like knowing he's jealous—that he doesn't like the idea of me with anyone but him.

I bite my bottom lip and tug on the hem of his black T-shirt. "Then we'd better get out of here."

Tyler leans in for one last quick kiss and then orders, "Get your legs inside."

He shuts the door and runs around to the driver's seat so he can fire up the truck. We instantly head back the way we came, and when we round the corner toward Granny's house, I tense.

"Where are we going?" I ask.

Tyler pulls into Granny's drive, but parks in the tall grass near the road, leaving us a good distance from the house. "I have an idea. Come on."

My shoulders slump as he gets out of the truck. He rummages behind his seat for a moment before shutting his door and then coming around to my side. Tyler opens my door and then chuckles. My disappointment must be evident. I'm not ready to go home. I want what he's promised to give me.

"Come on. I've got an idea of where we can go. We'll just have to be quiet." He holds out his hand to me while his other hand holds a folded-up plaid blanket. "Trust me."

I take his hand, giving him the trust he's asking for, and allow him to lead me toward the house. When he passes the house, the barn comes into view and it hits me exactly where he's taking me.

We sneak into the dark barn, and I'm suddenly uneasy about this idea. A flash of light comes from the spark of a match, and Tyler makes quick work of lighting a lantern that I never paid attention to before. "How did you know that was in here?"

The small flicker of light from the lantern shines on his face as he turns toward me, illuminating his features in the dark. "I saw it when we were out here cleaning the stalls."

I look around the barn. "What now? Don't say one of the stalls because I think my willingness the other day to have sex in there was a momentary lapse of my cleanliness judgment."

He shakes his head and then points above his head. "The hay loft—it'll give us the privacy we need and can make for a decent place to lay down."

He helps me onto the ladder and then follows up closely behind me with the blanket slung around his neck and the lantern in one hand. When I make it to the top, I take in the sight of the neatly stacked bales of straw. Tyler's right. Since we both live with our parents, there's not exactly a private place we can go to be alone, but this loft is a decent option.

Tyler sets the lamp on the floor and then spreads the blanket over a few bales of straw, making it almost appear to be a bed.

He turns and pulls me into him and then presses his lips lightly against mine, teasing me with what's about to happen next. "I've wanted you since that night in the parking lot, Avery. I know I said that we shouldn't do this, but I think it just might kill me if I don't have you. I know I'd regret it for the rest of my life."

Tyler's hand slides up under my shirt to touch the bare skin on my stomach, testing the waters with his gentle touch. His fingers inch up higher until they reach my breasts. The lacy material of my bra is all that separates him from me, and my breasts ache for him to touch them. I just want to feel him.

The way Tyler's taking his time with me allows me to get lost in how much I want him. I close my eyes and give in to what my body wants, and right now that's Tyler.

Tyler lays me down on the bed and then crawls up next to me and he cups my face as he kisses me again. Never have I wanted someone as much as I want Tyler. It's almost physically painful how much I want him. There's an ache inside me that I know only he can relieve.

I need him. Now.

My head falls back a bit as his lips trail down my jawline and then down to my neck. I moan as he threads his fingers into my hair and pulls my face back up to meet his. He crushes his mouth into mine and I throw my hands into that sexy blond hair of his.

"I'm going to make you so happy, Avery. I'll do anything for you," he says against my lips.

"You're already making me happy," I whisper.

He crushes his mouth against mine again and any politeness he had in his kissing technique is long gone. This kiss is more demanding, with the intention of not stopping with a little make-out session.

Tyler's nose skims my cheek and he inhales deeply as he unbuttons my jeans. "You have no idea how much I need you."

He helps me shimmy out of my jeans and then with one quick swoop, my shirt's off too. I lie there in just my bra and panties, and Tyler's lust-filled eyes rake over my body. He hooks his long fingers into the waistband of my panties and then slowly drags them down my legs. He then turns his attention to my bra and removes that as well.

The chill of the night air dances across my skin and goose bumps pepper my naked flesh. I lie there on full display before him, and Tyler doesn't hide the fact that he's studying every inch of my nude body.

He bites his lip while he stares into my eyes. "You are the most gorgeous thing I've ever seen."

My pulse pounds beneath my skin as I ache for his touch. The thoughts racing through my head all focus on how much I want him. Never in my wildest dreams did I ever expect for this to happen so soon. It's a little crazy and reckless but I can't help wanting this with him. Tyler leans down and kisses me, putting one knee on the straw bale bed. My lips instantly part, allowing access inside. The warmth of his tongue against mine causes an ache between my legs. I cup the side of his face, wanting nothing more than to feel his body against mine. Tyler mummers, "I can't wait to be inside this beautiful body."

My hand slips under the hem of his T-shirt and my fingers trace the distinct ripples in his stomach. I want nothing more than to see him.

As if he can read my thoughts, he grabs the back of his shirt and drags it over his head. The blond hair on his head flips out in every direction, turning his hair into a sexy disarray.

My tongue dances behind my lips as I trail kisses along his bare shoulders. When I reach the soft skin just below his ear, he moans in approval. I can no longer resist tasting him, so my tongue darts out, licking the salt on his skin. I pull back to look at his face and see a flash of hesitation in his eyes.

"God, Avery. I want you so much. Are you sure you don't want me to stop?"

I shake my head. "No. I want this. I want you to take me."

When those words leave my lips, it's like a fire gets lit within Tyler. Instantly, Tyler's over me, his bare chest pressed against mine as he devours my mouth with his. He quickly kisses his way down my chest. When his tongue swirls around my taut nipple, I pant and writhe beneath him. I love being with him like this more than I could ever have imagined, and he's barely gotten started pleasing me.

"Mmmm." A delighted moan purrs out of me when he moves on to the other breast, giving it equal attention.

He pushes himself up and then makes quick work of unzipping his jeans and kicking his boots to the floor of the loft.

He hooks his fingers around the waistband of his jeans and boxer briefs, and I feel the need to help him unwrap my present. I lean up and then pull the fabric from around his waist. His cock springs free right in front of me and my mouth hangs agape. His shaft is quite impressive and with it being right there in front of me, I do something that I've never done before. I lick my lips and grab the base of his length and ease the tip of him into my mouth.

Tyler sucks in a quick breath and says my name like a hiss before his fingers find their way into my hair. A reflexive gag happens the moment his head touches the back of my throat, causing my eyes to water a bit, but I keep going, quickening my pace.

Tyler moans. "Christ, Avery, I'm going to come if you keep that up, and I'm not ready to do that yet."

Understanding the signal, I pull back, freeing him from my mouth. Tyler grabs my legs and pulls me to the edge of our makeshift bed while wearing a wicked smile. "I think it's only fair that I reciprocate."

He bends down and teases me a bit by swiping his tongue across my lips. He slips his hand between my thighs and nudges them open. "Wider," he orders, and I comply without hesitation.

Tyler doesn't waste any time as my most sensitive flesh is splayed out in front of him. Tyler dips his head and then drags his tongue across my folds before focusing on my clit. He traces circles right in the spot where I ache to be licked the most and it doesn't take long before Tyler has me crying out his name as a wave of pleasure sends me over the edge.

Tyler lightly kisses the mound above my pussy, giving me a chance to calm down before he works a path up my body. "I love seeing you come. It's insanely hot. All it would've taken was a touch from you and I would've come while watching you fall apart like that."

Tyler crawls on top of me, and the weight of his body covering mine has me turned on yet again. "I can't wait to be inside of you. I'll probably come as soon as I slip in and feel this pussy milking me."

He slides his hand up my thigh as he hooks it around his waist. "You ready for this?"

I throw my head back and hiss out a yes as he slides his cock against my wet folds. My pussy is throbbing, begging for him to come inside. I'm not sure how much longer I can wait.

"Tell me that you're mine." He kisses my lips, and I taste myself on him. "Tell me, baby, that you belong to me."

I moan as every part of me craves him like crazy. I've never had a guy ask me to give him permission to claim me, but I like it. It's hot as hell and has me even more turned on, if that's possible. "I belong to you," I pant.

"Mine," he growls and pushes inside me.

The sensation of him inside me catches me off guard. I'm one hundred and fifty percent turned on and ready to go, but my body isn't as prepared as my mind. I claw his back as a whimper falls out of me.

It's been far too long since I've had sex. I had been working hard to not sleep around and I'm sure that's why Chance moved on to Charity—he was tired of waiting.

Tyler doesn't miss my momentary pain. His eyes jerk to mine, and all I see in them is concern. "You okay? Did I hurt you?"

I shake my head as the rest of my body relaxes. "I haven't been with anyone in a long time."

Tyler balances his weight on his elbows so he can study my reaction. "I thought you and Chance . . ."

I swallow hard. "No. It never got that far. I was trying to be good."

He drops his head, twists his lips, and then pops his head back up to meet my gaze again. "It's a little late now, but I should've asked if you are on the pill. I'm sorry. I was a little caught up in the moment to think about it."

He stares at me with questioning eyes and I shake my head. I can tell he's waging a war within himself, torn about what the right thing to do is, so I make it easy for him.

I stare into his eyes. "I want you—just like this—you and me with nothing between us."

Conflict is clear in his eyes, but soon he sighs and gives in, and begins moving inside me.

Neither of us turns our gaze away from the other. We both continue to stare at one another while our climaxes build. Sweat slicks Tyler's skin, and my hands slide up and down his back as he pumps into me.

His movements become more intense and I know he's getting close.

"I don't want this to end. Being inside you feels . . . damn, it feels so fucking good I don't even know how to explain it. All I know is that I want this forever—to feel you wrapped around me forever."

A tingle of pleasure shoots down my spine as his mouth covers mine and I teeter on the edge of another orgasm.

"Tyler," I cry out his name as another wave of pleasure rushes over me.

Tyler grunts as he quickly pulls out and comes all over the outside of my folds.

He presses his lips to mine one more time. "I don't think I'll ever get enough of that."

I smile and wrap my arms around his neck. "Me neither."

After getting dressed, I giggle as we make our way down the stairs. Tyler takes my hand and threads his fingers through mine as he leads me into the cool night air and back to the truck. Tonight has been perfect and I can't imagine how things can get much better than they are right now.

TYLER

It feels fucking amazing to have Avery on my arm and to know that she's mine. To know that it's been a while since she's had sex and she chose to be with me is a pretty big deal, and I feel honored she wanted to share that part of herself with me. Must mean she really likes me, and that only validates the feelings I've been wrestling with.

I was surprised to find out that she was so inexperienced, and I would've never guessed it had been over a year since she had sex. The way she was ready to smash Chance's headlights in made me believe they were a hot and heavy couple, but I was wrong. If I had to guess, that show she was putting on that night was more for those sorority bitches who left her stranded in a parking lot with a man she didn't even know.

I've officially staked my claim and I don't see how I can give her up now. I know that I went against my promise to Dad and slept with Avery, but I feel like if he were here, he would understand. I don't have any intention of fucking around, and I still plan on pursuing my musical aspirations.

Avery and I slink past her Granny's house on the way back to my truck.

We reach the passenger side of the truck and I open the door before I wrap my arms around her slim waist and pull her against me. "I don't want to let you go."

Her hands snake up my chest and then her fingers curl around my neck. "I'm not going anywhere."

She rises up on her tiptoes and presses her lips to mine. I close my eyes and get lost in how good it feels to be with this beautiful creature.

I pull back. "Come on before I take you back to the barn for round two."

She giggles as her hand slides down my cheek. "It's not a threat if the person will enjoy the torture."

A crooked smile crosses my face. "It's nice to know that I've left you thoroughly satisfied and hungry for more."

A blush creeps over her cheeks and I love that I affect her like that.

I sigh. "I need to get you out of here before I lose all my gentleman manners. You hungry?"

She shrugs. "Not really."

I raise one eyebrow. "Hmm. Maybe I didn't give you enough of a workout."

She brushes a strand of her dark hair out of her face. "It's not that. You know I don't like to eat much."

"You look amazing, Avery." My eyes trail down her body unabashedly and I have to say I like what I see.

"I . . ." She hesitates like she's trying to choose her words carefully. "I once had a bit of a weight issue and I have to work much harder than the average person to maintain my looks. I don't want to ever be the way I was. I don't ever want to go back to being ugly."

My heart crushes in my chest. "Avery, how could you believe that you've ever been anything other than amazing? When I look at you, I see a woman who other women would kill to be like. But even better than your looks, I know that you've got a good heart. Your father has told me how you have been the only person that's stuck by him since he lost his job. That tells me you're loyal, and that's a rare quality these days. The beauty you've got inside you trumps anything on the outside. So don't ever think for one second that you could look bad. You're beautiful. Even a blind man can see that, but it's what's inside of you that I'm falling for."

And there, I've admitted how I've been feeling about her and it wasn't awkward in the least. It seemed like she needed to hear me say that I like more about her than just her looks, and it feels amazing to finally voice to her what's been in my heart.

Her eyes glisten and I can tell by watching her expression that she's fighting back her emotions. That fight only lasts seconds before tears roll down her cheeks. "That's the kindest thing anyone has ever said to me."

"That's a shame, and I'm going to fix that. I'm going to remind you every day from now on how perfect you are." I lace my fingers through hers and then bring them up to my lips, kissing the soft skin on the back side of her hand. "I'm going to start by taking you out for a celebratory milkshake."

"What are we celebrating?" she asks.

She giggles as I hoist her up onto the bench seat of the truck and it's good to see her smile through the tears. I don't like seeing her frown, so I decide to keep her smiling by being a little brash. That always seems to get a reaction out of her.

I grin wickedly. "You and me fucking, of course."

She smacks me playfully on the chest. "I can't believe you just said that."

I chuckle. "I'm joking . . . partly. But in all seriousness, we need to get out of here. Wouldn't want your dad or grandmother to catch us."

She glances over to the clock on the dashboard. "It's nearly eleven. They've both probably been in bed for at least an hour now, so I doubt they've noticed us."

I smile. "All the same, I wouldn't want to explain to your father what we were doing in the barn. No father wants to find out the handyman he hired is fooling around with his daughter practically under his nose. No need to get him upset."

"Agreed," she answers. "I'm ready to head back to town when you are."

It takes us less than fifteen minutes to get back to town, where we swing through a local drive-through to grab a couple milkshakes, and then head back to Blake's place. His parties never stop on the weekend. There's not really a good bar for everyone to hang out at, so Blake's place has become the unofficial party spot for anyone close to our age.

When I park next to the curb, the first thing I spot is a crowd of people hanging out on the porch, which is typical for one of Blake's parties. The party tends to grow throughout the night.

I take Avery's hand and lead her back inside. The crowd in here is insane and there're more people in here than usual. This might as well be a dance club instead of Blake's house. These parties are the reason I refuse to be his roommate. I couldn't handle people taking over my home like this every weekend, but Blake thrives on it. He loves that people come here for this.

Blake tips his chin up when he notices us in the room. "You two get your fucking out of the way so you can actually hang out now?"

All the guys burst out laughing, and I can't even be mad at them. It was pretty obvious to everyone what we were doing based on the way I carried Avery out of here earlier, so it's natural that they'd give me shit about it.

I take their good-natured teasing in stride. I hook my arm around Avery's shoulders and pull her in tight against me. "Have you seen my girl?" I look down at her and grin. "She's beautiful. How can you expect me to resist her?"

Blake shakes his head and laughs. "Whatever, dude. She's hot. We all get it. You don't have to keep rubbing it in my face that I'll never have a shot at her. Unless . . ." He wiggles his eyebrows at Avery. ". . . she's into more than one guy at a time."

Avery wraps her arm around my waist and nuzzles into my side. "Sorry, Blake. I'm a one- man kind of girl."

It warms my heart knowing that this beautiful woman is with me.

I pull Avery in close and kiss her lips. "My girl. I like the sound of that."

She grins up at me, and just like that, I know I am such a goner for this woman.

We spend the rest of the night playing beer pong with Blake since that's the game of choice for him. When he beats us, he does a victory lap around the house and cheers, but then pouts like a baby when we win a game. I can tell Avery is having a lot of fun. It means a lot that Avery and Blake get along so well. Blake's been a really good friend to me and he was there when I lost my dad, so his opinion of any girl I date is important.

Avery lays the ping-pong ball down on the table and congratulates Blake on his victory before turning to me. "You ready? I need to get up early and clean the stalls."

I kiss the tip of her nose. "Let's go."

As we drive toward her house, Avery unbuckles her seatbelt and then slides next to me inside the cab of my truck. She lays her head on my shoulder and I pat her thigh. I'm really loving just being with her, and it's going to be difficult to leave her.

Rounding the corner down the dark country road brings a slew of flashing lights into view. My heart pounds in my chest the moment my eyes take in the situation. There're only a few houses on this stretch of road and Avery's grandmother's house is the one with all the commotion. The thick lines of trees in the heavily wooded front portion of the property prevent us from seeing what's going on until we get closer. I park beside the police barricade, and the raging fire on the other side of the trees comes into view.

"Oh, my God!" Avery screams as she jumps out of the truck and runs toward the driveway.

"Avery, wait!" I fling open my door and chase her—a million things going through my mind—and panic floods me.

Avery's met by a line of police officers blocking the driveway. She pushes forward while screaming "that's my house" over and over, trying her best to break free. It's then my eyes flick up the driveway and land on a horrific scene. The barn is engulfed in flames, completely unrecognizable, and the house just next to it has flames shooting up from its roof.

How the fuck did this happen? Things were fine when we were here a couple of hours ago. How could . . .

I stop myself in that thought as I retrace the last time we were here. The lantern in the barn—I don't remember turning it off. My mouth gapes open and my heart squeezes inside my chest.

This is all my fault—the fire—all of it. I was so caught up in fucking Avery that I left that fucking lantern going in a loft full of straw. I can't believe I was so careless.

It takes everything in me to not drop to my knees behind a frantic Avery, so instead I stare up at the sky. This is a message from my father. A warning that I broke a promise to him the second I started fucking around. My head spins. While Avery and I were alone in that barn, my musical ambitions were the last thing on my mind. She was my entire focus—not my future.

This fire—I don't like what it might be trying to tell me. We were the last people in that barn. It's unlike me to be so careless. I've put people I care about—Avery, her father and grandmother—at risk. I've hurt others because I haven't kept my focus where it should've been. I need to get my fucking shit back together.

"Where are they?" Avery's scream cuts through my thoughts and I can see that she's on the verge of losing it on the cop who is holding her back. "Tell me something, please! I need to know they're all right!"

I take a step toward her and wrap my hands around her shoulders and pull her back against my chest. A sob tears out of her as she turns and buries her face into my chest.

I hate seeing her hurt like this and it's goddamn ridiculous that no one is giving her a straight answer so I decide to give it a shot. I turn my attention to the stocky police officer in front of us. "Officer, please. Can you tell us where to find her grandmother and father? She just wants to make sure they're okay."

The cop frowns and pulls the hat off his head, revealing a buzz cut. It's then I notice he's pretty young for a cop—midtwenties, tops—so not much older than me. "Off the record, I can tell you that the only one I know about for sure is the older woman who lives here. She was taken to the hospital via ambulance after inhaling a lot of smoke."

"And my father?" Avery asks. "Where is he?"

"We're not sure. The elderly woman told us to check the barn, but at this time we've been unable to locate any male on the property—but they've been unable to get the flames under control in the barn, so no one has been in there to check it out."

"Oh, God." Avery's legs buckle below her and she grows limp in my arms as she begins to cry hysterically. "Daddy! Daddy!"

She can barely call out his name through her sobs.

My heart crumbles in my chest knowing she's going through hell.

"Miss, I know this is difficult, but we're going to need you and your friend here to step back—"

Avery narrows her eyes. "I'm not going anywhere until you find my father."

Instead of getting angry with her defiance, the officer's expression softens and he says, "We are doing everything we can, but right now what I need from you is to give the fire department and police officers the space to do their jobs. As soon as we locate your father, we will notify you."

She sniffs. "Okay. How about my granny? Is she okay?"

"From all the reports I've heard, she's being treated and they expect her to make it."

There's very little information being given, and it's probably because they really don't have anything to tell us.

The best thing I can do is pull Avery away and allow the crew here the space to work as they've asked. "Come on, Avery. We need to go check on your grandmother. Maybe we'll find your father there too."

She nods, but I know leaving here without knowing anything is killing her.

When we get back to my truck, she clings to me as she cries. I wish there was more that I could do to comfort her, but all I can do now is stand here and wrap my arms around her while I silently hate myself for causing her this pain.

AVERY

The night turns to day as the sun pops up over the trees, shedding light on the rubble of what was recently my new home. I haven't slept a wink because they haven't been able to locate my dad. I'm exhausted, both mentally and physically, but I will press on until Dad has been found. All night I've run the worst scenarios possible through my head, and I pray to God that none of them are correct.

I spent the night at Granny's bedside. Early this morning she regained consciousness and the doctors say that all signs point to her being able to make a complete recovery from this, which is a relief to know. I pressed her as gently as I could once she woke up about what happened and where she thought Dad could be, but Granny can't remember last night. She doesn't recall the fire. The last thing she remembers is going to bed, and then waking up here in the hospital.

I stare at Granny, who has fallen back asleep, and my thoughts drift to Dad. The need to find him is overwhelming and I can no longer sit here and idly wait for news. I need to go back home and see what's going on.

I nudge Tyler, who is asleep in the chair next to me. He hasn't left my side all night and I'm glad for that. I don't know what I would've done last night without him to hold me up while I fell to pieces.

Tyler's eyes snap open and then they focus on me. "You okay? Need anything?"

I lick my dry lips. "I want to go back to the house."

"Avery, I don't think that's a good idea."

"I have to be there, Tyler. I have to know one way or the other what's happened to my dad."

He frowns, and pauses for a long moment, before he gives me a subtle nod. "I understand. I'll take you back over there if you are sure you want to go."

"I need to be there, Tyler. He's my dad—the only one I have."

Tyler pushes himself up out of the stiff chair and holds his hand out to me. "Then let's go."

It takes about fifteen minutes to make it to the house. Fire trucks and police cars pepper the road and the driveway leading up to Granny's house. The same cop that asked me to leave last night is still on the scene. When he sees me approach, he immediately frowns and then comes to explain this situation.

The barn fire was finally put out just before dawn and the fire fighters began sifting through the rubble. The fire that started in the barn jumped over to the roof of the house because of the barn's close proximity. They were able to save the first floor of the house, so not all the contents inside were a total loss, but there is significant damage to the house and it's uninhabitable. It's likely everything will need to be demolished and rebuilt because the structural integrity of the building has been compromised.

The worry of not knowing where my father is keeps me glued here.

My hope is that somewhere in the confusion of the ambulance carting Granny away, Dad jumped in there with her and is waiting at the hospital for me. I don't want to allow any other possibility to enter my mind. There's no way that he's . . .

My mind trails off. I can't finish the thought. I refuse to even entertain the idea that anything bad has happened to him.

As hard as I try, a million things still rush through my mind, but the one constant question remains at the forefront of my thoughts: Why did this happen?

When I try to get Tyler to talk about what he thinks happened, he clams up and just shrugs, reminding me that the police and the fire department will figure things out. I think he's so closed off because he's worried too, but I give him credit. He's stuck here by me all night, holding me and allowing me to cry on his shoulder.

"Miss?" The cop tries to pull me out of the daze I'm in while thinking about all the things that could've happened to Dad. I focus my gaze on him, so he knows he has my complete attention. "The inspectors have recovered a body in the barn along with several animal remains."

The words slam into me like a ton of bricks and my knees buckle. My vision shifts and all of a sudden the world looks farther and farther away until everything goes black.

The black coffin is lowered into the ground and it's hard for my brain to wrap around the fact that my father is lying inside that box. Never again will I hear his voice or see his face, and when those facts cross through my mind I simply lose it all over again. I'm nowhere near ready to let him go.

I would do anything to bring him back—to hear his voice—and tell him how much I love him and make sure he knows how much he means to me.

I'm not ready to face this world without the man who has been a constant in my life.

There wasn't a big crowd for the funeral—mainly just people he knew locally. I didn't call anyone we knew from back home, except for Stacy, because most of them turned their backs on Dad when he needed them the most, so why would they be there for him now to pay last respects? I didn't even call my own mother. That may sound cruel of me, but I figured if she hadn't bothered to call and see if we were all right when we had to move out of our house, then she wouldn't care enough to find out about Dad . . .

I sigh deeply. It's hard for me to even admit in my head that he's gone.

Granny sits in the chair next to me, gripping my hand tight while her other hand holds a bunch of tissues. She doesn't say a word—she doesn't have to—but I know she's hurting too. Dad was her only child and she doesn't have any other family, so I'm all that she has left. All we have now is each other.

Tyler places his hand on my shoulder and gives it a comforting squeeze. He hasn't pushed me to rush out of the cemetery, but I can tell being here makes him uncomfortable. Now my father and his share the same cemetery as their final resting places.

I sniff and then blot both of my eyes dry with a tissue. I could sit here all day and stare at this hole in the earth, wishing hard that this was all a nightmare, but I know doing that won't change anything.

As much as it pains me to leave Dad here, I know I have to. All of the people who attended the funeral have long since gone, and the guys who fill the holes in have been standing outside the tent, waiting for us to clear out so they can finish burying my father.

I let out a shaky breath. "Are you ready, Granny?"

She sighs and then nods. "We should probably let them finish up here. Don't want to stick around and watch them cover him up."

I shudder at the thought, not wanting to see that either. I hold my hand out to her and say, "Do you need me to help you up?"

She clenches my hand and slowly rises up out of the metal chair, taking her time as her lungs are still mending and she's working on gaining her strength back. Tyler and I stand on either side of her, helping her to the car. When we get to the Mercedes, Tyler opens the passenger door and helps my grandma inside the car.

She pats his cheek. "Such a sweet boy."

Tyler gives her a sad smile but doesn't respond with words. Once she's situated inside, he closes the door and then turns to me. "Are you hungry or anything? I could take you to get something to eat if you'd like."

I shake my head. "I really just want to go ho—" I cut myself off, realizing my mistake. Granny and I don't have a home right now. The local motel is the closest thing we've got. "I'd rather just go back to the room."

He stares into my eyes for a long moment, and at first I think he's going to tell me something important, judging by the expression on his face, but he simply nods. "Then that's where I'll take you."

I let out a long sigh as he opens the back door for me, closes me inside, and then makes his way to the driver's seat.

None of us say anything on the way to the motel. All of us are lost in thought. My life has changed so much in the last couple of months but Dad was always my constant—the one thing in my life I knew would always be there. It's difficult to know that he's gone. I don't think I've even fully processed the finality of it all because I keep imagining that Dad's just simply gone on a business trip and that any minute he's going to show up and it'll be like nothing has happened. That this is all some wicked dream.

I look forward and I notice Tyler watching me in the rearview mirror. It's almost as if he's studying me for some reason and I can't figure out why. He's been different with me since the night of the fire. It may be because he's giving me space to process everything, but it feels like it's more than that.

We pull into the motel parking lot and park directly in front of our rooms. Tyler helps Granny out of the car and to her room. Once she's shut the door, he turns back toward me.

Tyler shoves his hands deep into his front pockets and steps up in front of me. "Are you sure there's nothing I can do for you before I go?"

"Go?" This catches me off guard because I fully expected him to come in and stay with me for a while—if not for the whole night. I need him to be here with me. I don't want to be alone.

He sighs. "Yeah. I thought it was best to give you some space."

"Tyler, I don't need space from you," I tell him like it's the most obvious thing in the world.

His lips twist and for some reason it appears that he doesn't like that answer. "All the same I feel like I should go."

I furrow my brow. "But I don't want you to."

He pinches the bridge of his nose. "Please, Avery, don't make this any harder on me than it has to be."

I flinch at that response. "Harder on *you*? If you haven't noticed, we just buried *my* father. How in the hell is this hard on you?"

"I know . . . shit, this is so hard." He shuts his blue eyes briefly and then opens them to refocus on me. "I'm leaving, Avery."

"Leaving? Are you fucking serious? How can you just leave me here when I asked you to stay? I need you."

He shakes his head. "I'm the last thing you need."

What he's saying . . . it makes no sense. "Tyler . . ."

"I can't stay. I can't ever stay with you again. Don't you see? All this—the fire—it's a sign—a sign that I'm not supposed to be with you. I was careless. I've hurt people. Your sadness is all my fault, and I swear I won't ever hurt you again."

"Tyler, stop." Tears stream down my face. "Don't do this. Don't put the blame for what happened on your shoulders. We both were in that barn. We both left the lantern—"

"No, Avery. It was my fault. I was losing focus on what I needed to do with my life, and bad shit happened because of it. It's another sign."

My mind jerks to the thought of Tyler's father and the promise he made to his dad. "You can't honestly believe all this happened because we slept together? Do you realize how insane that sounds, Tyler?"

Tears well up in his eyes. "Being together did cause this, Avery. Don't you see?"

I fold my arms across my chest. "I can't believe it. You're just like every other asshole who gets what they want from a girl and then ditches her." He tries to interrupt me, but I just keep going, raising my voice to the point where I'm practically screaming at him. "I thought you were better than that, Tyler! I thought you were a sincere guy. I can't believe that you're using my father's death to break up with me!"

"I'm not making this shit up, Avery! God, do you think I really want to leave you? That I never cared? Well, you're fucking wrong. I'm trying to do the right fucking thing here. I'm trying to do what's best for you. I can't stand the thought of you hating me, so I have to leave."

"I could never hate you," I tell him.

"You say that now, but once you've had time to see things clearly, you'll know this fire was all my fault." His lips pull into a thin line as a single tear drips down his cheek. "And you'll despise me as much as I despise myself. I have to do this, Avery. Being with you—it was a mistake."

My breath catches. "A mistake?"

He closes his eyes and when he reopens them, there's a hardness in them, like he's trying to cut off all his emotions.

"I have to refocus on my music, and there's no room in my life for you."

"No," I whisper. "You don't mean that."

"I do mean it. You were nothing but a distraction, Avery."

I clutch my chest, attempting to hold together pieces of my shattering heart. He's leaving me *now*?

My heartbreak turns to blind rage and I pull my hand back and lash out, smacking him as hard as I can. "You selfish son of a bitch. Of all the times to break up with me, you pick the day we put my father into the ground? I can't believe you'd do this to me. You're heartless and cruel and I never want to see you again. Do you hear me? *Never!*"

I turn and bolt toward my room, not giving him any more time to hurt me with his words. Hearing that he doesn't care enough to stay with me through one of the worst days of my life is enough to convince me that he isn't the man I thought he was. If this is how he operates, it's best he's leaving now before I spend any more time falling in love with him.

Part of me hopes that that smack will knock some sense into him and he'll come chasing after me, begging my forgiveness, but the other half of me knows that if he truly believes this was a sign from his father, then he'll leave me.

I make it through the motel door, slam it shut, and then lean back against it. I wait with bated breath for one of two things to happen—a knock at the other side of this door or the truck engine roaring to life.

The second the engine turns over in his truck, I know that he's not coming for me—that we are officially over and whatever I believed I shared with Tyler is now finished.

I slide down the wall and wrap my arms around my legs as I hold them against my chest. I drop my forehead down onto my knees. Tears flow and there's no use trying to stop them because I know from this moment on, nothing in my life will ever be the same.

AVERY

Over the next week, I spend a lot of time with Granny in her room to avoid being alone and thinking about Tyler or Dad too much. At night, there are no distractions to stop my mind from reliving the worst days of my life. Tyler hasn't called me, but I expected that much from him after the way he left me. There are so many things we still need to talk about, and I've worried about him a lot. I know he's taking the blame for what happened, but I wish I could've made him understand that I don't hold him responsible—that we both left that lantern on, that we both share in the guilt.

I wish I could talk to Tyler, but I'm afraid to call him. I'll give him time and when he's ready to come back to town, we'll talk.

I lie on the bed and listen as Granny makes countless phone calls to her insurance company about getting money to rebuild her home and barn.

I can't believe how many hoops you have to jump through in order to get the money that you're entitled to.

As that thought passes, my cell rings. I grab it off the bed and the name on the caller ID makes me sit up straight as a board. It's my mother.

My heart leaps in my chest. I haven't spoken to her in months and I can't imagine what in the world she'd be calling me for after all this time. From what I gather, she's been pretty content with her new life and pretending that she doesn't have a family that she ran out on when things got hard.

I press the green button and answer.

"Avery? Hi, darling, how are you doing?" Her voice is smooth as silk and it makes me edgy.

I debate whether or not I should tell her about Dad. I doubt she would care that he's dead seeing as she didn't care enough about him to stick by his side when things got tough. It's probably best to keep the conversation light and get a feel for why she's calling me now.

"I'm okay," I reply.

"That's really good to hear," she answers. "I just heard through Stacy that your father passed in a fire. Why didn't you call me? I would've liked to pay my respects. I was married to the man for nearly twenty-two years."

That's just like my mother—to make dad's death all about her. I would like nothing more than to fire at her all the reasons why I didn't contact her about Dad, but I decide against it. I'm sure my words would fall on deaf ears. I remain quiet and allow her to ramble on.

"You know you can stay with me if you'd like until you get on your feet. Jack has plenty of room, so I'm sure he won't mind that you're here."

Jack . . . the doctor she left Dad for. The thought of living with her again doesn't tempt me at all. She's the last person I would even consider running to.

"I'm fine staying here with Granny. We're working on getting everything rebuilt."

She's quiet for a few moments, but then says, "You're a lot like him, you know. Your father was always so stubborn. It's one of the things I loved most about him when we were young. I loved how he never wanted to settle and always pushed for more because he wanted a better life for his family than what he had growing up. He couldn't wait to get out of Wellston."

"It's not so bad here," I say as I think about the few interactions I've had with the locals around here. "People for the most part are friendly."

"Sure, they're nice, but there's nothing there. You could benefit so much from returning to school and finishing your degree, finding a respectable guy with good prospects to marry, and really starting a life."

Anger boils inside me, and I'm instantly brought back to the times when Mom tried to control everything about me. This is the first time we've spoken in so long and yet she's still trying to dictate the best way for me to live my life when she doesn't even know me anymore.

I've changed, and I'm not about to go back to being the stuck-up bitch she was trying to turn me into.

"You know what, Mom? I'm not going back to school—or at least not until I'm good and ready. I like it here. I like spending time with Granny and I think I'm going to stay here with her."

"Avery, don't be silly. Now that your father is gone and my attorney informed me that your father made you the sole executor of his will—"

Things instantly begin to click. "Is that why you called? Are you trying to figure out how to get the last few pennies that Dad had to his name? Divorcing him wasn't enough? You have to try and take what little bit he has left? News flash, *Mother*, all he had left was his Mercedes, and if that's what you're calling to get, that's too damn bad. I'm keeping it."

"Avery! Don't you dare speak to me that way! I am still your mother, and I think it's only fair seeing as I was the one who encouraged him to get the life insurance policies that I get half of—"

I grip the cell so hard in my hand, it's a wonder it doesn't snap in two. "Shut the fuck up. You left him! He loved you and you left him like he meant nothing to you when things got tough. You don't deserve a goddamn penny! If I'm in charge, I'll see to it that you don't get a dime, so don't ever call me again, you greedy bitch."

I slam my thumb down on the "End Call" button and throw my phone on the bed and growl. That woman is far worse than I ever thought. "What in the hell did he ever see in her?"

Granny lifts her eyebrows. "I think my boy was blinded by her beauty."

"I never want to be like her," I admit out loud.

Granny cradles my chin in her hand. "You could never be like her. You've got too much of your father in you—a good heart. You care about more than just yourself." She sighs. "I don't like that she's upset you so much. What the hell did she call for anyway?"

"Money, of course. It sounds like she wants to get her hands on Dad's life insurance policy and she has to go through me to do it, seeing as how Dad made me the executor of his will."

Granny smiles. "My boy was smart. I should've known he had things covered for tragic situations like this. Even when he's not here, he's taking care of you."

I give her a tight-lipped smile. That is exactly like him—always making sure that I have everything I need.

Tears burn my eyes at the thought of never seeing him again. "I can't believe he's gone, Granny. He's gone and the only thing my mother cares about is money. I hate her."

A sob rips out of my throat and Granny instantly wraps her arms around me as we sit on the bed together. I'm not sure what I'm going to do, but I know I've got a long battle ahead of me.

TYLER

I roll over on the couch and pull the pillow tighter around my head, trying to block out the sound. This was one of the main reasons that I didn't want to move in with Jimmy, but given the short notice, what choice did I have? I hadn't planned on moving to Columbus until I had saved up enough money for a deposit on my own apartment, but I knew I couldn't stay in Wellston where I would run into Avery.

It took everything in me to start that truck and drive away, knowing that she was already having a day from hell. I didn't want to leave her, but I knew there was nothing else I could do. I'm no good for her. Bad shit will continue to happen to me and everyone I care about until I get on the path I'm supposed to be on, and staying with her would just bring more complications into her life that she doesn't need.

It was a dick move to leave her the way I did, but I knew if I stayed with her in that motel room, I wouldn't have had the strength to leave her, and I would've ruined both of our lives.

The woman screaming Jimmy's name while he fucks her senseless cuts through my pillow earmuffs so I decide it's best if I go wait outside on the patio of the apartment until they're done. I can't stand listening to her screeching voice.

Hopefully he'll get rid of this one soon. He met her at the gig we played tonight, and he never stays with the barflies for more than one night.

I push myself off the couch and grab my T-shirt off the floor and pull it over my head before heading for the sliding door. I step out into the cool night air and flop down in the lawn chair that's on the tiny patio. A notepad sits on the little table next to the chair, so I pick it up, moving Jimmy's cigarettes and lighter to the side, and read the lyrics Jimmy scratched down. My eyes scan the words and I attempt to sing them in the same tempo that's playing on repeat in my head.

It doesn't take long before I come up with an entire musical accompaniment to go along with the words.

It's not half bad, and if Jimmy would use the arrangement I've put together, I can see the song really coming together.

I tap out the beat of the song on my thighs with my thumbs and just as I come to the end, the sliding door opens behind me.

I turn around in my chair in time to see Jimmy poke his head out the door. "It's safe to come back inside. I just sent her packing."

I laugh at my crazy friend. "I take it that one isn't a keeper?"

Jimmy shakes his head and comes out and plops down in the chair next to mine. "I gave up a long time ago trying to find a good one, man. I think finding one perfect woman you want to settle down with is nothing but a fucking myth."

My mind drifts to Avery. Good women do exist—they're just really hard to find.

Jimmy grabs his cigarettes off the table. The orange flickering flame from the lighter illuminates his face as he lights one up. "What do you think?"

I glance down at the notebook in front of me. "It's good, man. I think with a few adjustments to fit the beat I just came up with, the song will be stellar."

He takes a long drag and then blows a puff of smoke between his lips. "Let's hear what you've got."

I begin tapping the beat out on my legs.

Tap. Double-Tap. Tap. Tap.

I open my mouth and sing along to the beat, never chancing a glance in Jimmy's direction. The words of the song connect with me on such a personal level. It's about a guy who is in love with a girl that he can never have. To Jimmy, I'm sure these lyrics apply to his latest Hollywood crush, but for me, there's only one face I see—Avery's.

When I'm finished, my gaze flicks over to Jimmy. He's always been a hard one to read, but the smile on his face means one of two things: Either he's about to bust my balls or he thoroughly approves.

I nervously await his decision either way.

"I like it, Tyler," he finally says. "It's all emotional and shit—which is exactly the vibe we always go for. The chicks will really go for it."

"Thanks," I answer while relief floods me. "I think you should sing it tomorrow night at our next gig."

Jimmy shakes his head, and the long hair on his head swishes around his face. "I don't think so, man."

"What? Why not? Aren't you tired of doing nothing but covers? I think if we throw in an original song or two every now and then we can test how well the fans are going to respond to the song. It might be the thing that pushes us to the next level."

"No. No. What I meant to say was I think *you* should sing it tomorrow night."

"Me?" I question. "Why should I sing it? It's your song."

"Just because I wrote it doesn't mean that I should be the one to perform the song. People write songs for other people all the time. You connect with this song on a much deeper level than I do, obviously. It makes you feel something. I could tell that by the expression on your face when you sang it. I wrote the song about a car, not about a woman, so it definitely doesn't drudge up the same emotion in me as it does you." He chuckles for a second but then points his finger at me while his gaze grows serious. "You . . . you sing it like you're in love with a woman. You make it believable and that's what validates any song."

I rub the back of my neck, suddenly nervous that Jimmy can see through me so easily, but I know he's right. Performers have to be able to make their audience believe them. It's what takes a good song and turns it into something great, but I'm not sure if I'm ready to expose that side of myself to the world.

"I see those wheels turning inside that skull of yours," Jimmy says. "Don't overthink this like you do everything else. Just trust me on this one. This song was meant for you to sing. I can feel it. It's like the stars are perfectly aligning and shit, pointing you to a greater destiny."

I laugh and shake my head. "You and that fucking destiny talk shit, makes you sound like a fucking hippie."

He smiles. "If this were the seventies I would most definitely be involved in the whole peace and love movement."

I push myself out of the chair. "All right. I'll do it, but I'm playing drums on this one, and we have to get the rest of the guys together and practice that shit. I don't want to get up in front of a crowd and fucking butcher the first original that we ever do."

Jimmy grins. "Will do, chief."

I shake my head as I go back inside the apartment. Perhaps this is a sign that I'm back on the path that I should've been on all along. It appears that I'm only supposed to have my music—that there's no room for love while I'm on this road. I would be thrilled that I'm doing what I set out to do if I could only block out the fact that I may have just sacrificed the love of my life to do it.

I twirl my drumsticks in the air as nerves rock through me. The crowd in this college bar is rowdy tonight. It makes me nervous to sing any love-related songs because it's obvious these people are only here to drink and find someone to take home.

We spent all afternoon practicing the original song that Jimmy wrote, and I have to admit after a few hours, we sounded decent—not perfect by far, but definitely decent. Things really came together. I just hope that we don't make complete assholes out of ourselves and butcher such an amazing song.

Jimmy turns toward me and nods. "Count it off, man. You got this."

His vote of confidence in me renews my spirit to perform in this crowded bar.

I click my sticks together and kick off the beat. "One . . . two . . . three . . . four!"

The bass drum echoes around the room and I follow up by banging my snare and hi-hat in perfect rhythm. I glance around the room and there are a few heads nodding, and when the other guys join in playing bass and lead guitar, things come together just like they did during our rehearsal.

I lean in toward the microphone and lick my lips before I open my mouth and sing the first verse of the song.

I see you waiting . . . waiting for me.
You don't know how bad I wish we could be . . .

I close my eyes and picture Avery's face. It's not hard for me to picture myself standing in front of her begging for forgiveness because in my mind I've pictured it a million times. But no matter how many times I can see the scenario in my head, I know I can never attempt to make it a reality. Getting Avery back will only be a fantasy for me because I'm sure she hates me, and I don't blame her. I would hate me too if I were her, but it doesn't change that we weren't fated to be together. Music is my mistress and I have to learn to give her my entire heart and push Avery out of it.

After making it through all the verses in the song, I sing the closing line and open my eyes when the roar of the crowd erupts in the bar.

Jimmy's wearing the biggest shit-eatin' grin on his face as he turns around to face me. "Fucking told you!" He quickly turns back around and addresses the crowd. "We're going to take a quick break. Don't forget to tip your bartenders!"

We all hop down from the stage, practically floating on cloud nine because we stepped outside our comfort zone and it appears to be a huge fucking success.

"That was unbelievable! Did you hear how much they loved that song!" David, our bassist, crows while his dark hair flops in his face. "I think we need to come up with more originals!"

"Agreed," Jimmy says. "It feels pretty damn good that they seemed to like that so much."

"I'm going to get a round of drinks to celebrate." I smile and slap Jimmy on the back and head toward the bar.

The place is crawling with people. I snake my way through the bodies and finally push myself up to the bar. After waiting a couple minutes, a beautiful blonde wearing a tight, low-cut black dress turns around on her barstool and notices me standing behind her. She doesn't try and pretend that she's not staring at me as I wait on the bartender to get to me.

The blonde licks her lips and then traces her exposed cleavage with her index finger. "Hi. You looked great up there."

I nod and try not to seem rude. "Thanks."

She tosses her hair over her shoulder. "You sounded pretty good too."

I give her a tight-lipped smiled and thank her one more time. This doesn't seem to appease her. I suspect her invitations to flirt don't often get rejected, because blowing her off only seems to make her even more determined.

She leans into me and places her hand on my forearm. "Is your girlfriend here?"

I shake my head. "No."

I don't even bother telling her that I don't actually have a girlfriend, because it doesn't really matter because I'm not the slightest bit interested in pursuing anything with her. I don't do random sex.

"I don't usually do this," she says and I have to fight the urge to roll my eyes. Here we go. "I find you extremely attractive. Do you want to come back to my place for a nightcap and perhaps a little dessert after the show?"

I highly doubt that she doesn't usually do this. She just straight-up asked me to fuck her far too easily for this to be one of the few times in her life that she's asked a man to have a one- night stand with her.

I sigh and as bad as I want to blow her off, I know it won't be good for the band if it ever got out that I was rude to someone at a show. Instead, I decide to redirect her to a place where her offer might be gladly accepted.

"Sounds fun, but I can't do it." I turn and point over toward Jimmy. "See the guy with dark hair over there?" She nods. "That's Jimmy. He's the front man of our band and I'm sure he'd love to continue to party after the show with you."

Her eyes move from me to Jimmy and then back to me. Her eyes trail over my forearms, pausing to study the ink on my arms before her eyes flick back up to meet mine. "Too bad. You bad-boy types are usually a damn good lay."

She doesn't give me time to say anything else before she pushes up from her stool and sashays toward Jimmy. Just as I thought, Jimmy's face instantly lights up when the blonde approaches. I knew that she would be right down his alley.

"That was decent of you." I turn back around and notice an older redheaded woman standing on the other side of me. Her bright red hair matches the red top she's got on, and she most definitely stands out here among the crowd of twentysomethings that pack the bar. "I take it that you're a team player?"

"Always am." I scratch the back of my neck and hope that this lady isn't about to hit on me too.

"That's good to know," she says and then hands me a card. "I'm Jane Ann Rogers, a talent recruiter for Mopar Records. I'm working on putting a band together and I'm looking for a drummer with a decent voice to sing backup. If you're interested, give me a call and we'll talk more about it. I think you'd be a great fit to go along with the other two guys I've recruited."

I stare down at the card I'm pinching between my fingers and it appears to be very official. This might just be the big break we've been waiting on. I can't wait until I can tell the guys.

"Thank you, Ms. Rogers. I'll speak with the guys and let you know."

She shakes her head. "No. This offer doesn't extend to them. Only you. If you're interested."

I lick my lips and glance back toward the band. This feels wrong, but how many times in my life am I going to get an opportunity like this thrown into my lap? If things work out and I play along with whatever this project is, maybe down the line I can bring Jimmy and David into the business with me. I know they would jump all over this offer if they were me.

If I don't take this talent scout up on this offer, sacrificing Avery will be for nothing. I'm not sure what my dream really is anymore, but I know that I'm committed to this musical path because I've destroyed any hope of ever winning Avery back. I have nothing else going in my life, so this woman's offer sounds pretty damn good.

"I'm interested. Thank you."

Her face lights up. "You made the right choice. Hope you're ready. Your life is about to change."

A wicked smile stretches across Jane Ann's face, and it makes me wonder if I've just made a deal with the devil.

THREE YEARS LATER . . .

AVERY

I wipe down the bar one more time and sigh. It's been a long night and the crowd doesn't seem to want to go home. I glance over at Blake, who has busied himself talking to a group of women who have been sitting at the bar all night. I've grown quite fond of Blake over the last few years, and he's become one hell of a good bouncer for the bar Granny helped me open when I decided that I wanted to stick around Wellston and look after her. She helped me realize that I can be a successful business owner, even though I'm young. I found it only fitting to pay homage to Granny with the name of my bar: Granny's Poison Apple.

Thanks to the life insurance money Dad left me, I was able to buy a small building in town and renovate it. From the old brick façade outside, it doesn't look like much, but it's one hundred percent mine. It's been a steady stream of income for me over the last couple of years, and I'm thankful for that.

It's been a challenge to be successful in this small town, but I think my hard work has really begun to pay off because it's now the place where everyone in town comes when they feel like having a drink. Blake really helped me out in the beginning by bringing his weekend parties to the bar instead of just keeping everyone at his place. He helped to validate the bar as the best night spot around, so it was only fitting that I give him a job.

I glance up at the clock on the wall and notice in fifteen minutes it'll be two in the morning. "Hey, Blake, could you let everyone know it's last call?"

He nods and smiles at me. "Sure thing, boss lady."

He cups his hands around his mouth and shouts, "Last call!"

A big guy, whose thick salt-and-pepper beard complements the black leather vest he's wearing, yells back, "It's last call when we fucking say!"

My eyes snap over to the group of guys sitting at the corner table. It's a well-known fact that they are part of a local motorcycle club that has a reputation for doing things on the shady side of the law. They're not regulars, but I have seen them in here from time to time.

Blake's stance stiffens and he rolls his shoulders back. My gut twists and I've come to know that Blake doesn't back down from threats, which is why he's such a phenomenal bouncer, but I can't allow Blake to get tangled up with these guys. "Blake," I call his name over the music that's playing on the jukebox and he turns in my direction. "Let it go. Come help me clean these last few glasses so we can get out of here as soon as they're done with their drinks."

Blake takes a step in my direction and then freezes when the man in the corner yells again. "Go do as you're told, boy!"

I gasp, knowing that since this threat is personal, there's no way of calming Blake down now.

When he turns, all I can do is yell his name from behind the bar in hopes it will be enough to deter him from confronting the men. "Blake!"

It's no use—he's across the room and standing in front of the table full of guys before I even have a chance to come from behind the bar.

Blake leans down and balances his weight on his fists so he can stare the big man right in the face. "Finish your drinks and get the hell out of here."

The even tone of his voice presents a calm front, but I can tell by the way his muscles tense beneath his T-shirt that he's seconds away from losing his cool with these guys. The fact that Blake's outnumbered three to one doesn't seem to faze him either, but it scares the shit out of me. I just wish there was someone to back him up.

The man narrows his eyes. "You better watch how you talk to me, boy. I'm not a man you want to make upset."

Blake straightens his stance and meets the stare of the menacing man on the other side of the table. "I don't give a fuck who you are, but it's time for you to go."

The biker stands up slowly and the other two men flank his side. "Who's going to make us? You?"

The three men chuckle like a funny joke has just been told.

"That's right." Blake balls his fists up at his side. "Don't make me throw your ass out of here."

The man throws back the last of his drink and then sets the beer bottle back on the table in front of him. For a second it looks like the men are about to leave without making a fuss, but out of nowhere the leader of the group sucker punches Blake from across the small table.

Blake staggers back, shakes his head, and then dives over the table, taking himself and the man to the floor. The sound of glass shattering and the commotion of the table and chairs falling to the floor turns every head in the place. The other patrons quickly flee from the bar, leaving me alone with the fighting men.

The other two men reach down and drag Blake off of their companion. Blake struggles in their hold as the other man pushes himself to his feet. Panic floods through me. I can't just sit by and watch these goons hurt my friend.

I jump on the back of one of the guys and wrap my hands around his neck, yanking back as hard as I can to get him off Blake.

The man grabs a handful of my hair and slings me off his back. "You little bitch!"

He leers at me and out of the corner of my eye, I see the other two men taking turns punching Blake. My heart races as I slide back on the floor to get away from the guy. He narrows his eyes and just as he begins to reach down for me, someone rushes his side and tackles him to the ground.

It takes my eyes a moment to focus on who just saved me, but the moment they land on a familiar face, I gasp.

It's like seeing a ghost.

Tyler holds the man down and punches him in the face, knocking the man unconscious. Once the guy is down for the count, Tyler turns his attention to the two men beating on Blake. Tyler grabs a handful of one of the guys' shirts and lands a hard right square to the nose. This frees Blake up to fight the other man, and now that it's an even two-on-two match, the bikers no longer have the upper hand.

Tyler and Blake work in unison, and once they have control of the situation, they drag each of the bikers toward the door and throw them out one by one before locking the front door of the bar.

I take a moment to check Blake's face. Blood drips from his nose and there's a pretty decent-size gash over his right eye. "Are you all right?"

His tongue darts out and he licks the corner of his busted lip. "Yeah. I'm good." He turns his attention to Tyler, who stands there watching us curiously. "Damn, man. You've got some kick-ass timing. Thanks for jumping in there and saving my ass."

Tyler grins and holds his hand out to Blake and they join hands and do that weird guy handshake-hug thing. "Anytime. When I first walked in, I wasn't sure what in the hell was going on, but when I saw Avery jump on the one guy's back, I knew shit was out of control. I figured you guys wouldn't be opposed to me jumping in and knocking some heads around to help out."

Hearing Tyler say my name brings back a flood of old memories. It's been three years since I've seen him in person.

Tyler's gaze shifts in my direction and my breath catches as I try to think of something to say to him.

The reunion is cut short, because minutes after the bar is empty, red-and-blue lights shine through the window. I open the door and the cops quickly jump out of their cars, running toward the men who are stumbling around in the parking lot.

"Freeze. Get down on the ground," one of the officers shouts at the bikers.

Tyler and Blake flank my sides as two of the officers work on detaining the men we just kicked out while another man in uniform approaches us. He's a short man, with a stocky build, whose dirty-blond hair pokes out beneath his hat. I've met him a few other times when I had to call the police to break up a couple fights in the bar.

"Avery," the cop greets me.

"Good evening, Officer Ryder."

I'm not sure if it's a good thing or not that we know each other's names since he needs to come to my place of business so often.

"We had a report that there was an altercation here. Can you tell me what happened, Avery?" He clicks his pen and is ready to write down my side of the story.

I clear my throat and begin explaining how we were trying to close up and Blake announced last call, and how those particular men refused to leave, and then engaged in an altercation with my bouncer.

He nods and makes some notes on a pad of paper he has in his hands and then turns his attention to Blake. "Would you like to press charges?"

Blake folds his arms across his broad chest and shakes his head. "No."

I'm surprised by his answer because if I were Blake I would want those assholes prosecuted to the full extent of the law, but Blake being Blake, I suppose he sees pressing charges as a weakness.

The cop sighs. "All right then. If you're not pressing charges, then we'll have to let them go."

"Understood," Blake says. "There's nothing about those assholes that I can't handle should they decide to come back and try that shit again."

"Have it your way." Officer Ryder turns to me. "I'm going to release the suspects. If they come back, you call us, Avery. We don't want things getting out of control again."

"I will," I reply and he smiles.

Officer Ryder returns to the other cops, who are detaining the bikers. I can tell by the way he keeps nodding toward us that he's explaining to the bikers that no charges are going to be filed. Soon the men hop on their bikes, fire them up, and then pull out of the parking lot.

As soon as the parking lot is clear, the cops get into their cars and drive away too.

I turn to Blake and inspect his face a little more closely. Everything appears to be angry and swollen, the busted lip and the cut over his eye being the worst of the damage. "Let's get inside and get some ice on that."

Blake doesn't argue with me. Instead he turns to head inside and holds the door open, waiting on Tyler and me to follow.

I glance up at Tyler and I find myself utterly confused. On one hand I'm excited to see him and on the other I still harbor a lot of resentment for the man. It's been three years since I was last with him— three years since Dad died and everything in my life changed. I know we weren't together long, but I expected Tyler to be there for me.

But, as I stand there looking at him now, I realize none of that matters. All of it's in the past. We are strangers to one another. He's no longer the nice country boy that I met a few years ago. He's Tyler White of Wicked White—one of the hottest rock bands in the country. Hell, the band even made him change his last name from Mercer to White. He's a completely different person.

I followed his rise to fame from the time Wicked White released their debut single until they became the band with the highest-grossing tour of any musical act last year.

It's nice to know Tyler's dream came true. This man before me is a superstar. It's exactly what he left this town to accomplish and the reason he shoved me out of his life. Tyler's eyes soften and he opens his mouth to say something, but before he gets a chance to, Blake's voice cuts between us, "Yo, you two coming or what?"

"Yeah, we're coming," I say and then turn to Tyler and decide that I need to let things be, if only for tonight. "Come on. Drinks on the house for saving our asses tonight."

Tyler smiles and then follows me inside.

TYLER

Sitting across from Avery is like something out of a dream. I knew coming back here that it would be a possibility that I would run into her. I just never imagined that it would be so soon. When Blake asked me to meet him at the bar where he works tonight, I had no idea that Avery would be there too.

Blake adjusts the towel that's wrapped around a bunch of ice on his face. "So, Mr. MTV, how's life been treatin' ya? I saw you on TV when you went to the Grammys. Life must be pretty fucking sweet for you."

I chuckle. "You could say that."

Same old Blake—hasn't changed a bit since I saw him last. Sure, we've kept in touch through texts and social media, but being around someone in person is a much different experience.

Blake takes a long pull from his beer. "Is it true what they've been saying on the news? That the front man for your band is missing?"

I pick at the label on my bottle. "It's true. No one has heard from Ace White since he walked off stage a week ago."

"So that's why you're back?" Avery asks as she studies my face. "You're on a bit of a break?"

I nod. "Yeah. Since they can't find Ace, my tour manager, Jane Ann, cancelled all our upcoming tour dates. I figured it would be a good time to come back and visit Mom and—" I slap Blake on the back. "—a few old friends."

I don't admit to her that deep down I was hoping that I would see her too because I'm not sure how she would react. I still haven't forgiven myself for her father's death, and if I can't do that, how can she possibly forgive me? On top of all that, I ran in her greatest moment of need. No matter what my personal reasons were for doing that, I'm ashamed I put my own fears ahead of her needs. I wasn't strong enough to stay and face her. I caused her pain and then made it worse by running. I don't deserve any kindness from her.

"Do they have any idea where the guy went? I mean, I'm sure they have to have some leads. It's not like one of the biggest stars in the world can just go into hiding—staying undetected. He's pretty famous to not be recognized."

I sigh. "You would think that, but neither Jane Ann nor the cops have any leads on his whereabouts."

Avery frowns. "Do you think it's possible that he's dead?"

"God, I hope not. I don't really get along with the guy, but I wouldn't wish anything bad to happen to him."

She tilts her head. "Is he close with anyone in the band?"

I shrug. "Ace doesn't really get along with anyone in the band. He's way too controlling and doesn't allow anyone else to have any creative input. It's like he doesn't trust that we were picked by the label for this band because we have talent too. It's a shame, really. I think if all the guys ever put their heads together and started creating some real music—not just the canned music they have to record—Wicked White could really be something."

"Being the biggest band in the world isn't enough for you?"

I shake my head. "It's not about being the biggest or the best—it's about creating music that we're all proud of. Every guy in the band can sing and we all come from different backgrounds. I think we could each bring something unique to the table."

"Why don't you just go out on your own then, since it seems they are stifling you creatively?"

"It's not that easy. These big record labels . . . they just don't hand out record contracts—not to guys like me who are looking for solo gigs. They signed me up for their band, and I figure if I play by their rules for a while, maybe they'll give me a solo shot down the road."

"Makes sense, I guess. It's like you're working an entry-level job and just biding your time for your promotion."

Her analogy is pretty on point.

I give her a small smile. "Something like that."

Blake downs the last of his beer and sets his bottle on the table. "Shit. I'm fucking beat. I think I'm ready to head home and hit the bed. You still staying with me tonight, Tyler?"

I nod. "If that's still okay with you."

"Of course it is. What are bros for?"

"Awesome. Thank you. Seemed too late to go to Mom's tonight, so I appreciate you letting me crash."

Blake stands and then pitches his empty bottle into a nearby trash can. "Sweet. Then I'll see you there in a bit. You remember where it is?"

"Yeah."

"Okay, cool. Then I'll leave the front door unlocked for you." Blake leans down and kisses Avery on the top of her head. "Later, boss."

I know I don't have any right whatsoever, but seeing Blake kiss Avery, even in such an innocent way, makes me jealous as hell. I've thought about her every day since I left. I often wondered what it would've been like for us if the fire never happened that night. How our lives would've been different. I've missed her. If I ever admitted how much I missed her, people would probably classify me as certifiably insane since our time together in the past was so short.

"Later, Tyler!" Blake calls over his shoulder as he heads out of the bar.

Silence wraps around us the moment Blake closes the door, leaving Avery and me alone in the bar. The quiet is almost deafening and I feel like I need to say something.

So many times at night I would lie awake and imagine the things I would say to Avery if I were ever given the chance to apologize to her for the way I left her, but right now, sitting across from her, all of the fancy things I'd planned to say won't come to mind. Instead, I can only remember one word, and I feel like I need to just say it so she knows I mean it.

"Avery, I'm sorry about how I left you. I was—"

She holds up her hand, cutting me off. "Tyler, please. You don't have to apologize."

"Please let me do this, Avery. I owe you this."

She shoves herself away from the table and then stands, busying herself by clearing off the table. "It won't change anything, Tyler. Sometimes it's best just to leave things be. Things were going so good before and now you have to go and ruin it by bringing up old, hurtful memories."

"I didn't mean to hurt you, Avery. I was scared and blamed myself for all the bad shit that was happening to you."

My career took off so quickly and I got swept up in it. Focusing on the music helped me escape the guilt I feel about Avery's father and the way I treated her. Music is the only thing that has brought me any joy since I walked away from Avery, which really reinforces the sense that I am supposed to fulfill my promise to Dad.

"Do you even hear yourself? The fire was an accident."

"But it wasn't! I caused that fire because I left the goddamn lantern burning in the barn and I would've never done that if I hadn't been sneaking around to fuck you. Had I listened to my father—your father would still be alive—and God, I am so sorry for that! At times it feels like I killed him."

Avery covers her mouth as tears stream down her face.

I don't mean to yell at her, but I'm so overcome with emotion that I can't seem to control my tone. The therapist I've been seeing for the past year—when the guilt of what happened began affecting my every-day life to the point I found it difficult to function—told me that it would be good to have a conversation with Avery. I'm pretty sure my not being able to control my emotions when it did happen wasn't a part of that plan.

Truth is? When I think about Avery losing her father, it brings up all the raw emotion of when I lost mine. It was difficult to relive that so soon and it was like losing my father all over again. My head got all con-fused and I didn't handle the situation with Avery the way I should have.

"Stop." A sob rips through her. "I've thought about that night every damn night for the past three years, racking my brain on all the what-ifs. Don't you think I blamed myself too? We both forgot the lantern that night—not just you—and I've been beating myself up over it every day since then. This didn't happen because your dad cursed us. It hap-pened because it was an accident.

"I've spent so many sleepless nights worried about you—worried about how you shouldered all the blame yourself—but I never heard from you again, so I figured you didn't need my comforting."

My heart is crushed in my chest. Here is a girl who has every right to hate me, and yet, she's trying to ease my pain.

"Avery . . ." She presses her fingers to my lips.

"You don't have to say anything else. I've already forgiven you. I had to in order to forgive myself."

"I don't expect anything from you," I tell her honestly. "But I would very much like to start over with you and be friends."

She stares into my eyes. "We can do that as long as you promise not to run off and avoid me for another three years."

A huge weight lifts off my chest. It's hard to believe the things I've struggled with for the past three years are so easy to talk about. Maybe it is because I'm in a much better place now, with a more rational thought process.

I give her a sad smile. "Deal."

She lets out a big sigh of relief. "Now that the elephant in the room has been squashed, how about another drink?"

"Sure," I say, but then feel compelled to ask, "Blake won't mind that you're out with me so late?"

She furrows her brow as she pops the tops on two beers behind the bar. "Why would he care?"

"Aren't the two of you a thing?" I'm not sure if I really want to know the answer to that, but I need to know what kind of situation I've just walked into.

If my best friend has been dating the girl who's held my heart for the past three years and keeping it secret, I might just lose my shit on him.

She laughs. "God, no. We're just friends. Blake helped me get this place going and is really my only friend in town. What made you think that we were together?"

I shrug. "You're beautiful and Blake—let's just say I know him. I figured he would try to get with you once I was out of the picture."

She walks over and sets my beer in front of me. "Well, you're right about that. He did try, but I made it clear very early on that I didn't think about him like that. He bucked the whole idea of being just friends but he eventually came around. He's a really good guy and I'm not sure what I would've done without him for the past three years."

I nod, but guilt and jealousy washes over me again. It should've been me being there for her, but I'm happy that she had someone. "I'm glad he was there for you."

Avery traces the condensation on her bottle with her index finger and for a long moment she doesn't say a word. It's like she's lost in deep thought and her mind is elsewhere. Then she totally catches me off guard. "Would you like to come over for Sunday dinner tomorrow? Granny's making fried chicken and I think she'd love to see you."

Her offer wasn't one I expected but I'm grateful for the invitation "I'd love to. What time should I come over?"

"Dinner's at six, and don't be late or you'll have to deal with the wrath of Granny."

I smile, and for the first time since I left this town, I feel a little bit at peace over what happened when I left Avery at that motel.

After I help Avery clean up the rest of the bar, I drive through town and make it to Blake's house. He's still driving the same old Mustang, and it's parked in front of the house. I kill the engine of the Kia rental car I'm driving and head up the sidewalk toward the front door. The knob twists open and it's unlocked just like he said. All the lights are off, so I just set my bag down by the front door and then lie down on the couch. How exhausted I am doesn't actually hit me until that moment. Within minutes I fall into a deep sleep and I don't move a muscle.

It's not until beams of light come through the window and shine right in my face that I wake from my death-like sleep. I yawn as I stretch my arms over my head. It's been a long time since I roughed it on a couch, and I'd forgotten how hard it is for my six-foot frame to fit on one all night.

I push myself up and balance my elbows on my knees as I scrub my hand down my face. I pick up my cell phone off the floor and notice the battery is about dead as I check the time. It's after twelve, so I've already slept most of the day away. I've got to haul some ass if I want to make it over to Mom's house before I go to Avery's for dinner.

I rummage through my bag, find my charger to plug my phone into, and grab a quick shower. I towel off and then dress in a pair of jeans and a T-shirt before exploring the house, looking for Blake, who has been uncharacteristically quiet this morning. He's probably still trying to get in some beauty sleep to calm down that mess of a face from the fight last night.

The biker took a few good shots before I made it in there to help Blake out.

I push open the door to his bedroom, and there's no sign of him. His bed is unmade, but that's not unusual. I've never known Blake to be the bed-making type. The next place I check is the kitchen, but there's no sign of him there either, so I figure he probably already left for the day. I mean, just because I'm here as his guest doesn't mean that he needs to report to me where he'll be all the time.

After that thought, I head to the living room and collect my duffel bag, along with my cell, and head out the front door, locking it behind me. It's then I notice that Blake's Mustang is still parked out front of his house. Now this puzzles me. He isn't one for riding with others because he insists on driving his baby everywhere.

I pull my cell out of my pocket and dial Blake's number, but it goes straight to voice mail. "Yo, Blake, it's Tyler. Give me a call when you get this. I wanted to see what your plans for the evening were. Later."

I end the call and then stuff the phone back into my pocket before jumping into my rental.

The drive to Mom's doesn't take me long, and the moment I pull in the driveway, I immediately feel comfortable. This little yellow ranch house, no matter how old I get or how far away I live, will always feel like home to me.

I step out of the car and gravel crunches under my boots as I walk the path to Mom's front door. I twist the knob on the front door, but it's locked. I furrow my brow. That's odd. She never locks her doors, especially if she's expecting someone.

I knock on the door. "Ma, it's me. You in there?"

The rustling on the other side of the door, and then her undoing the locks, tells me she knows I'm out here.

The door swings open and my petite, blond mother has a grin on her face from ear to ear. "There's my boy! It's so good to see you." She wraps her arms around my torso and squeezes me in a tight hug. "It's about time you came home to see your mama!"

I chuckle. "It's good to see you too, Ma." I step back and inspect her. "You cut your hair?"

She flips her short blond locks around with her fingers. "You like it? I thought it was time to change things up a bit."

"It suits you," I tell her and then glance around the house to find that nothing else has changed. I frown when I notice the same furniture that's been in her living room since I was a kid is still present. "Where's your new furniture?"

She waves me off dismissively and heads toward the kitchen. "I told you to stop sending me money. I refuse to spend a dime of it."

"Ma, how many times are we going to fight about this? That money is to take care of anything you need." I follow her into the kitchen, where I'm greeted with the smell of her famous pot roast and my stomach rumbles.

"Baby, you should be saving your money instead of giving it away."

"I'm not giving it away. I want to make sure you're taken care of. If Dad were here, he would have no problem letting me do this for you."

"If your Dad was here, he would've whooped your butt for running off like you did in the first place."

"I highly doubt that," I tell her. "He made me promise him that I would get out of this town as soon as I could and go after my music dream."

"He might've done that because he wanted to see you go experience more than we ever did, but he never meant for you to avoid where you come from. He didn't want you to avoid this place either. Not seeing your mother in three years is a travesty."

I sigh and rub my forehead. My mother is a stubborn woman and when she's made up her mind that things should be a certain way, that's how it is. There's no changing her view. Like now. I know she's upset with me for not visiting in all this time, but I was too afraid to come back here and face Avery. I wasn't ready to face the guilt and shame. It took me a year's worth of therapy to realize that if I didn't come back here and deal with my past, I could never really move on.

I offered to fly Mom out to see me while Wicked White was on tour, or even when we spent some downtime at our homes in California, but she always rejected the idea. Mom's fear of flying limits a lot of things for her, visiting her only child being a crucial one.

I know the only way to make her happy is to promise to change all that. "I get where you're coming from, Ma. From now on, I'll make sure I come out and see you way more often. How's that sound?"

Mom smiles. "That sounds like a good plan to me." She takes the lid off the crock pot and stirs the roast beef around a bit. "Hope you're hungry. I haven't cooked this much in a long time."

"Starving." I laugh and hug her and kiss the top of her head. "Let's eat."

I spend the rest of the afternoon with Ma, telling her all about my adventures on the road and about the process in the studio when we cut albums. She listens like it's the most fascinating stuff in the world.

I've missed spending time with her, and she's right, I need to make sure I see her more often.

When I glance down at my phone, I notice two things. One, that it's nearly five thirty so I should head on over to Avery's place to have dinner with her and Granny, and two, that Blake still hasn't returned my call, which is unlike him.

I push myself up from the comfy couch in the living room. "I need to take off. I'm going to go have dinner with an old friend while I'm in town."

A knowing smile fills her face. "Would this be the same mysterious someone you used to see a lot before you left?"

I laugh, amazed at her memory. "I can't believe you remember that."

"Honey, I'm your mother. I remember everything about you." She hugs me one more time. "Be careful out there. This town has gone to shit in the last few years. The crime rate—well, let's just say nothing's safe around here anymore."

Her locked door springs to mind. "Is that why you were barricaded in here earlier?"

She nods. "I'm a single woman, living in the country alone. Can't be too careful nowadays. Be safe."

"Always am," I tell her as I head out the front door and to the car.

It doesn't take long for me to make it to Avery's driveway. My fingers curl around the steering wheel and I grip it tight to try to ignore the awful memories of the last time I was here. I turn down the driveway, and soon the house comes into view, only this time it's twice the size I remember it being and it practically looks brand-new. I'm guessing after the fire, this place was a total gut job. The house is wrapped in new white siding while new windows add to the curb appeal. When my eyes slide over, just right of the house where the barn used to be, I'm relieved to see only a patch of grass where it once stood.

I park next to the house, beside the Mercedes. The car reminds me of Avery's father, and I have doubts about being able to handle going inside the house where he used to live.

It hurts to know that I was so self-centered that I didn't stick around to be there for Avery when things got tough for her—for the times when she needed me the most. I wasn't strong enough to be there for her then, but I'm praying that all the soul-searching I've done since I left will help me find the strength to be here for her now, for as much as she will let me.

Avery opens the screen door and she pokes her head outside and waves me in, so I know sitting in this car and debating if I can make it through this dinner is out.

I hop out of the car and grab the bouquet of flowers I picked up on the way over for Avery's grandmother as a thank-you for the dinner she's fixing tonight. I won't know what to do when I go back onto the road after having all these home-cooked meals. I won't be able to stomach fast food again for a while.

I make it to the top of the third step on the porch and Avery greets me by holding open the screen door while wearing a smile. "You made it."

Her relieved tone sets me at ease. Maybe just like last night, this dinner will be easier to get through than I anticipate. The only thing that will cause me to lose my shit right now is a lot of talk about her dad.

I step inside and the place is almost as I remember, only with hardwood floors throughout the house and more modern furniture. "Wow. It really looks nice in here."

She nods. "Thanks. We like it."

"Looks like they got that addition done too," I add.

"Oh yeah, we just had them include the construction cost of adding a new bedroom to the renovation budget, so it worked out quite well."

A high-pitched, shrill scream erupts from the back of the house, which catches me off guard. I wasn't aware this was a family event. "Are there more people here than just you and Granny?"

Avery twists her pouty pink lips. "You could say that."

"Oh," is all I say. "If you're having family over, I don't want to impose."

"Don't be silly, Tyler. You're our guest of honor."

"I—I am?"

"Yes. Now come on. We don't want to keep them waiting." Avery takes me by the hand and pulls me through the house, but stops me just short of reaching the kitchen.

She pauses for a moment to take a deep breath.

I give her hand a squeeze. "You okay?"

She turns toward me and sighs. "I'm sorry. I thought I could do this, but I don't think I can."

There's a change in her demeanor. She's gone from overly happy to see me to apprehensive.

I furrow my brow. "You're not making any sense, Avery. Can't go through with what?"

She opens her mouth to say something, but quickly closes it as two little bare feet slapping against the wood floor come charging toward us.

A little girl wearing a pink dress stretches her hands up into the air as she runs toward us. Her two blond pigtails bounce as Avery scoops her up into her arms. "Momeeee. Whet's eat."

"We have to wait a minute, Maddie." Avery's voice softens when she speaks to her. "I want you to meet someone special. Can you tell the nice man, hello?"

Maddie looks at me, smiles, and greets me. "Helwhoa."

My mouth drops open as I stare at the little girl who is now in Avery's arms. She can't be more than two or three years old, but I'm not really good with kids' ages so that's a total guess.

Avery stands there, holding the girl, while staring at my face, gauging my reaction. I don't know what she expects me to say. Once I quickly do the math, it takes me back that she would have a child with someone else so quickly after I left, but I'm in no place to judge her for her actions.

"She's beautiful," I tell Avery.

"Thank you. I think she looks a lot like her daddy." Avery's eyes meet mine and for some reason I just know.

There's a ping of acknowledgment down deep in my gut that hits me hard in that moment. It's not difficult to figure out why Avery was so nervous moments ago and nearly changed her mind about me staying for dinner.

I might as well ask the obvious question that I know Avery's waiting for me to say.

I lick my suddenly dry lips, as I stand there still in shock. "Is she . . . *mine*?"

Avery swallows hard, then nods. "Yes."

"How . . . When . . ." So many questions rage through my mind that I don't even know where to begin, but I can't hold back the biggest question on my mind. "Why didn't you tell me about her? Didn't you think I had the right to know that I had a daughter?"

"Of course I should've told you." She bites her lower lip. "I guess I was afraid that you'd reject her like you did me and I couldn't risk my little girl's heart getting crushed like mine did. I'll do anything to protect Maddie, but she's getting older and now that she's beginning to talk pretty well, she's been asking more and more about you. She deserves to know her father. You and I both know how important a father is."

Those words are like a solid punch to the gut and make me feel even more like a piece of shit for leaving than I did before.

"Avery . . . I'm . . . I . . ." It's hard for me to express exactly what I'm feeling.

I'm angry with Avery for not telling me about our daughter, but I'm also scared shitless that this little girl in front of me now owns my heart completely and she doesn't even know me yet.

But that's going to change. From this point on, I'm going to be there for her—for both of them.

"I know this is a lot, and I want you to know that I don't expect anything from you. I just wanted you to meet her." Avery reaches over and places her hand on my forearm. "Come on. Let's eat and I swear I'll answer any question you have."

Desperately needing answers, I follow her into the kitchen while attempting to reconstruct the shattered parts of my mind and wrap my head around the fact that I'm a father.

AVERY

I fully expected Tyler to go ballistic on me once he discovered I've kept our daughter a secret from him. I know I would've gone nuts if I were him, but I hope he understands that I did what I thought was right at the time. I was afraid of him hurting Maddie if he ran out on her someday like he did on me.

His life seems so busy, and I'm not sure how much time he'll have for her, but at least now the decision is on him. If he chooses not to be a part of her life, I will understand. It will hurt like hell, but I won't force him to be around her if he doesn't want to be.

I've been supporting the two of us for years, and I plan on keeping that up no matter what happens. I like standing on my two feet, and proving to myself that I can be an independent woman. That's really important to me because I don't want to be anything like my mother.

Going back to school was no longer an option those first couple of years after my little girl was born. Luckily Granny was there every step of the way with me. She's taught me how to be a good mother—how to really take care of someone other than myself. She and I have raised Maddie together.

Granny's at the stove, pouring all the food out of pots and into bowls. She turns and notices Tyler standing there.

A smile crosses her face and she opens her arms to him without any reservations. "Aren't you a sight for sore eyes? It's good to see you, honey. I hope you're hungry because I went all out today. We've got fried chicken, mashed potatoes—the works."

Tyler laughs. "I'm starving and it sounds amazing. Between you and my mom, if you guys keep feeding me like this, I'll be five hundred pounds when it's time for me to go back out on the road."

Granny waves him off. "Pfft. Now you're startin' to sound like Avery when she first came here a few years back—worried about maintaining her girlie figure. Ain't nothing wrong with having a little meat on your bones. It's healthy. It took me a while to convince Avery that it was okay to eat more than a goddamn salad."

"Granny," I scold her while I set Maddie down in her booster seat and push her up to the table. "Language."

Granny grimaces. "Sorry. Old habits and all that are hard to break. I've been doing my best though to cut out the cursing completely now that we have a little set of ears takin' in everything we're sayin'."

Tyler laughs because he's been around my granny enough to know that's no easy feat for her. I think her favorite word in the world is *damn*.

I chuckle to myself as I turn around and grab the plate of chicken off the counter and place it on the table.

"Is there anything I can do to help?" Tyler asks me.

"We got this, but it would be great if you could keep Maddie entertained until we're ready."

He bites his lip and looks hesitantly down at the daughter he's only just met. It's like he needs a bit of reassurance to talk with her. "You sure?"

I smile. "Of course. You're her father. She'll love getting to know you."

Tyler pulls out the chair next to Maddie and sits down next to her. "Hi, Maddie. How are you?"

"Good," she answers but never really looks at him as her eyes are trained on the lock-and-key toy sitting on the table in front of her. She bites her tongue—something she's been doing more and more of lately as she focuses on whatever task is at hand. She tries to stick the key in the lock, but it won't budge. "Fix it, Daddy."

My eyes widen and my heart does a double thump behind my ribcage. The use of the word *daddy* is so natural that it takes me back a bit.

Tyler's eyes widen and then flick up to mine. "Did she . . ."

I set a bowl of mashed potatoes on the table. "She did."

"How did she know that I'm her dad?"

I stare down and watch Maddie as she continues to work on the toy in front of her. "When we were getting dressed for dinner, I explained to her that she would be meeting someone special, and when she asked me who it was, I simply told her that she would be meeting her daddy. I never dreamed that she would call you that right away."

"Child's smart," Granny says, butting into our conversation. "Hopefully even smarter than you two."

"Granny," I warn, not ready for her to start preaching to us about all the mistakes Tyler and I have been making and how we haven't been fair to Maddie. "Now's not the time. I didn't invite Tyler over here so you could give him the third degree."

"It's not just Tyler who needs to hear what I've got to say—both of you have done a lot of wrong, and I think it's high time you work out some way to fix it."

"That's what I'm trying to do, Granny—fix everything. It was wrong of me to not tell Tyler the moment I found out I was pregnant. I know that's how you feel, but at the time, I thought I was making a good choice by not telling him."

"Well, you were wrong. Both of you. You were wrong for not telling him and you—" She flicks her gaze from me to Tyler. "—You were wrong for just leaving her behind like that. Did you ever plan on contacting her again to see how she was doing with everything?"

Tyler's face blanches. "I meant to, but I didn't think she would want to hear an apology from me so soon after I left, and I was too busy running to hear what she had to say to me. The passage of time doesn't make me any less sorry for what happened though."

She nods. "That's good to hear. Now that you've both admitted that you were wrong for ending things the way you did, the two of you can start working things out. You both need to get on the same page and stick there for the sake of Maddie. The little angle deserves the best from both of you."

I sigh, and as many times as I've heard similar speeches from her over the last three years, it doesn't make hearing it again this time with Tyler any less impactful. She's always been right—deep down I've known that.

"She's right," Tyler says. "We need to figure this out. I want the opportunity to get to know her—to be a part of her life—so I'm willing to do whatever it takes to make things work between us, Avery, so we can both be there for Maddie."

"Daddy, fix it," Maddie says to Tyler while holding up the pink plastic lock and key.

Tyler takes the toy from her tiny hands and sticks the key into the slot and then twists. "There you go."

Maddie squeals with delight as the latch opens up and swings free from its locked position. "Yaya! Daddy fixed it!"

We all clap and focus our attention on the little girl who has completely stolen all of our hearts.

AVERY

Most of the dinner conversation tonight was centered on Maddie.
I love seeing Tyler take a genuine interest in his daughter and it
makes me feel guilty for not telling him about her sooner. It's obvious
now that I see the two of them together that he's going to be a great father.

I stand up and grab my plate along with Maddie's and put them on
the counter next to the sink.

Granny smiles over at Maddie and says, "Let's take a time-out for
a potty break."

The two of them scamper out of the room and I'm left with just Tyler.

He stands up and carries his plate to me. "She's amazing. You're
doing a good job with her."

That's nice to hear from him and it makes my heart extremely
happy to know that he wants to be a part of her life. "I'm so glad that
the two of you have hit it off so well. I can't tell you how nervous I was
about bringing you here. I wasn't sure how you were going to react to
the news."

Tyler nods and then runs his fingers through his shaggy blond hair.
"I'll admit, you caught me off guard, but I've been trying to really keep
my temper in check and not run off when things get a little too hard."

"That's good to know. Hopefully that means you'll be coming around more often."

"I'll be here to spend time with Maddie every chance I get—and maybe even with you, if you aren't opposed to that."

I bite my lower lip. "I'll admit that I held a lot of anger toward you until Maddie actually got here. She taught me a lesson about how special the bond is between a child and their parents, so it helped me understand a little more about why keeping your promise to your dad was so important to you—no matter how crazy it sounded to anyone else."

"Me leaving Wellston had nothing to do with you, Avery. I hope you know that. It had everything to do with me and my own fears and guilt. I couldn't understand why you didn't hate me and blame me for the loss of your father. I never imagined that you shared in that guilt with me. I wish I would've known that you felt that way. I would like to think even as fucked up as my head was back then, that I would've been here to comfort you and make sure that you knew that it wasn't your fault—that you had nothing to feel guilty over—but honestly I was so raw about Dad's death back then I'm not sure that knowing that you felt guilt too would've changed the way I reacted."

"I could say the same thing to you," I remind him. "I think if we'd communicated with each other a little more, everything would've been different."

He leans his hip against the counter as he faces me. "We could wrestle with the what-ifs forever, but that won't do us any good. It'll only continue to make us hurt. Back then, I was just so sure that I was being punished for breaking my promise to my dad and that I was not only going to bring myself down, but I would've taken you down with me. I couldn't imagine anything worse happening than causing your father's death."

"But that's where you're wrong, Tyler. You weren't punished. Don't you see? That night we were together may have turned into a tragedy, but something extraordinary came from it, too, and she's got little blond curls and is the best thing that's ever happened to me."

"I wish I could've been here for you. Maybe it would've made everything else feel a little less tragic if I had stayed behind and seen the good that came from that night. I'm sorry that you had to go through it all alone, and I understand why you didn't trust me enough to tell me about Maddie. The only thing I can ask for now is a chance to prove my loyalty to you and her."

Tyler reaches up slowly and softly touches my cheek. "I'm sorry I left you, Avery."

Tears sting my eyes as I lean into his touch and I know this road isn't going to be an easy one. Trust is a hard bridge to mend. I just pray that he really has changed like he said.

Tyler wraps his arms around me and pulls me into his firm chest. We don't say anything else—we don't need too. We've said all we can and the only thing we can do now is move forward from this point and do our best to prove to one another that we've both learned from our mistakes.

"Can I take you out tomorrow night?" Tyler asks. "I want us to start over."

I nod. "I'd like that."

He smiles. "Great."

The next day Tyler shows up promptly at six. It reminds me of old times when I come bounding down the stairs to meet Tyler. It's nice to feel like we've picked up where we left off even though we both seem to have grown up quite a bit since the last time we saw each other.

I open the passenger door of the car and hop inside. "Hey."

Tyler smiles at me. "Hey, beautiful. Hungry?"

"Starving."

"I know just the place." He winks at me.

When Tyler pulls into the drive-in diner that we used to frequent when we were together last, I'm immediately transported back three years, before everything went up in flames.

After we order, we spend the entire time catching up on what we've missed in each other's lives. He tells me all about touring with Wicked White and how being a musician hasn't been like he imagined. He doesn't have any creative freedom when it comes to the kind of music they make. The record label creates all the music and lyrics, leaving the band members to perform as directed.

It doesn't seem like he's very happy with his current situation.

"Why don't you quit?" I ask.

Tyler takes a bite of his sandwich and shrugs. "I've wanted to for a while now, it's the only thing I've got going for me. I've got nothing else."

I reach over and lay my hand on his arm. "Maybe someday you'll find what you're looking for."

Near the end of our meal, our conversation turns to Maddie. I love that Tyler's so interested in learning everything he can about his daughter.

"Blake's going to be so happy when I tell him about everything," I say. "He's been hounding me to tell you about Maddie since the day she was born."

"I'm glad the two of you are friends. He's a good guy to have by your side in tough times. He's a loyal dude." Tyler sighs. "Speaking of Blake, do you know where he might be? I called him earlier today and he's still hasn't gotten back to me."

Avery shakes her head. "No. The bar is closed on Sundays and Mondays, so I don't typically see him, but knowing Blake he's found some chick to bring home."

Tyler twists his lips. "That's the thing. He wasn't at his house this morning when I drove by there earlier today. I spent last night at my

Mom's, and he still hadn't contacted me, so I drove over to his place and knocked on his door. It was really strange, considering his car was still parked out front."

"He didn't mention any plans with anyone today when you spoke with him last?"

"I've not seen him since the first night I got here and we fought with the bikers," Tyler admits. "When I got to his house that first night, it was so late. I literally walked in his front door and crashed on his couch. I didn't even bother changing my clothes because all the lights were off and I didn't want to move around a bunch and make a lot of noise in case he was asleep."

"That's strange," I say. "Maybe we should go to his house and check out the place."

"You'll come with me?"

"Of course I will. Can we make a quick stop at the bar? He might've been dropped off over there or something and just stayed since his car hasn't moved from the driveway."

"Has he done that before?"

I shake my head. "Well, no, but he does have a key and it makes logical sense that if he's not at his place, then he might be there. It's worth it to stop and check."

"Okay. Sounds like a plan."

"Great. Do you mind driving me back home so I can tuck Maddie into bed before we head out to look for him?"

"Of course not."

When we arrive at Granny's we head into the house. I turn to Tyler and say, "Give me a few minutes to make sure Granny is fine watching Maddie while we go out looking for Blake. I'll be right back."

"Hey, Avery? Would it be okay if I come back there with you and tell Maddie good-bye before we leave?"

I smile and love the fact that she's at the forefront of his mind. "Sure, come on."

We make our way back to Maddie's room, and I notice Tyler smile.

"This would've been the addition that your dad and I were working on."

"Yep. I wish Dad had been around to see it completed. He would've loved the way it turned out."

We come to the first open door in the hallway. "This is Maddie's room. She loves playing in here. She's a typical little girl—dolls are her world."

He chuckles. "I'll take that as a hint when it comes time to buy her some gifts."

Maddie is on the floor playing tea party with her dolls while Granny sits on a chair in the corner. Tyler stands beside me and just observes her in action for a few moments before Maddie glances in our direction and notices us.

"Momeee and Daddy, wanna play tea party with me? It's realwe fun."

Tyler grins and the expression on his face practically begs for a little extra time to have this moment together with our daughter.

I walk into the room and kneel down next to Maddie. "We have time for a cup."

"Yaya," she cheers and then instantly goes into setting out two saucers and teacups for us. "Sit down, Daddy!"

"Yes, ma'am." It's cute that Tyler obeys her the way he does.

We finish up our imaginary cups of tea and when I get clearance from Granny, Tyler and I say our good-byes and then head over to the bar.

The ride over to the bar is filled with Tyler's questions about Maddie. He explains to me that since he's missed so much, I have to tell him everything about her. We're talking every single detail from her birth to what went on with her today.

We pull into the parking lot and Tyler cuts the engine. "I know I've bombarded you with questions, and I'll probably ask you a million more until I feel like I'm up to date with all things Maddie, but I do have one more and then I'll give you a break for a bit."

I laugh. "It's not really a hardship talking about the apple of my eye. Maddie is my favorite subject in the world."

"I can see why. I can't seem to get her off my mind."

"She tends to have that infectious personality. I think she's destined to be a star."

His smile widens. "There's no doubt about that. Anyone who meets her is going to fall in love. She's beautiful, like you."

My heart does a double thump after hearing his compliment. "Tyler . . ."

He leans in to me, and if I move even a fraction of an inch, our lips will meet. It's been a long time since I've kissed Tyler, and I wonder if kissing him would still give me the butterflies like it used to.

"I've only got one more question," he whispers.

"You can ask me anything."

"What's Maddie's last name?"

"Mercer, like you. I know I should've asked you first, but—"

"I love that you gave her my name."

"I'm glad."

Tyler leans in and presses his lips to mine. They're soft yet commanding, just like I remembered, and it makes me crave more.

"I've missed you so much. You don't know how many nights I dreamed about tasting these lips again. This can't be real," Tyler whispers.

So many times I've thought about being in Tyler's arms again. I can't believe this is actually happening and that he knows about Maddie. I never imagined in my heart of hearts that things would work out like this. Even though I was mad at him, I've missed him.

My fingers reach up and trace the shaggy hair on the top of his head. "Believe it. We're very real—and we make really pretty babies together."

"That we do."

This time when we kiss it's not gentle like it was only moments before. This time I can feel the urgency in his lips as they tangle up, like if he doesn't take me right here and now in this car, I'll disappear. A hunger that I haven't experienced since the night I was with him comes over me and more than anything else right now, I want him. I want Tyler to take me.

"Do you want to go inside?" Tyler asks, waking me from my daze. "They'll be more room inside."

I nod while the fire inside me still rages. "Come on."

We all but run to the front door of the bar once we're out of the car. I flip on the lights and then lead Tyler to my office in the back.

I close us inside and Tyler yanks his shirt over his head, revealing his chiseled body and the vast array of tattoos covering his body. Looks like he's added a few more to his chest since the last time I saw him.

I swallow hard, still unable to look away from his body. He notices me staring, and his smile turns wickedly sexy. Tyler starts toward me like a tiger stalking his prey, slow and deliberate. His approach causes my stomach to knot. I sit on my desk.

Tyler sits beside me and twists around to look into my eyes. "What do you say, Avery? We have the bar all to ourselves . . ."

I giggle at his playfulness.

He cups my face, leans in, and kisses me.

I've missed this.

I've missed him.

I close my eyes, and allow my fingers to find their way into his hair. He's got sexy hair. Tyler kisses down my neck and when his lips meet the soft skin under my ear, the scruff on his chin tickles a bit. From that point he moves on to my shoulder, placing soft kisses on my exposed flesh. He slides the straps of my tank top down and I throw my head back when he kisses my collarbone.

My chest heaves as the need to kiss him again consumes me. I grab his face in both of my hands and pull his mouth back to mine and I kiss him like I need him more than air.

Tyler stands up and pushes himself between my legs.

"I've missed you so much. I know I don't deserve a second shot at your trust, but I'm begging you for one. Avery, I love you," he says.

I bite my lip as I stare into his eyes. All I see when I look in them is truth—that he means what he's saying. Our connection has always been strong but he broke my heart once and I'm afraid to give it over to him again.

"I . . ." I hesitate.

Tyler brushes a strand of hair away from my face. "It's okay if you don't say it back. I have to earn that from you, but I want you to know that I'm willing to put in the work. I'll do whatever it takes to prove to you that I meant it when I said I love you and that I won't ever hurt you again. I've learned my lesson. I can't be without you."

I nod, feeling thankful that he understands why I can't say the words back to him just yet.

He starts to slide my straps back up, but I place my hand on his, halting it in place. "Just because I can't say it doesn't mean I don't feel it. I still want you, Tyler—more than ever."

That is all the permission Tyler needs. He grabs the hem of my shirt and pulls it up over my head. His large hands glide down the length of my torso and I shiver with anticipation as he reaches for the button on my shorts. I grind against him, loving the feeling of his hard cock pressing against the spot that is begging for his touch right now.

He pops the button open and unzips my jean shorts. The moment his mouth touches the base of my throat, a moan escapes me as he caresses my breasts over my lace bra.

"Mmmm, just as nice as I remember," he says after he pushes down the fabric of my bra. My nipples pucker as his bare chest rubs against them and he kisses me once more before he bends down and wraps his lips around the taut pink flesh.

I arch my back, loving the way his mouth feels on me. "Tyler . . ."

"I want you to be mine," he murmurs and then swirls his tongue around my nipple. "I need you in my life."

He pulls me up to a standing position and then slides his hand down my stomach and into my panties. When his fingers flick across my wet folds, I shiver. "God . . .Tyler!"

"Please, Avery. Say it," he commands, his breath hot against my skin.

"I'm yours. I always have been," I admit in a breathy tone, not feeling the least bit self-conscious because it's the truth.

"I love you, baby. I want to make you feel so good," he growls and then flicks my clit.

"Tyler," I cry as he touches me. "Oh, God."

"So wet," he whispers. "I want to bury my cock inside you."

Tyler dips a finger inside of me and I moan as I arch against his palm. He works his finger in and out of me a few times before slipping in two fingers. My heavy panting fills the otherwise silent room as he brings me to the edge of orgasm.

He pulls his fingers out and rubs a circle over my clit, and I nearly explode on the spot. I want him so much right now, and I need those pants off of him. I reach for the button on his jeans and shove them down along with his boxers. He is ready for me, hard and standing at attention. I grab the base of him and stroke. He moans and lets out of string of soft curse words before dropping his head forward as he continues to finger me.

Sleeping with him goes against everything I've been telling myself I would do if I ever saw him again, but it feels right, as if there's nothing else that matters now but him and me.

Need builds inside me and I'm anxious to have him deep inside me, thrusting hard. A tremor erupts through me as I come hard.

Tyler lifts my chin, and claims my mouth with his as he pushes me back onto the desk. He reaches down and pulls his wallet out of his pants pocket before retrieving a gold foil package. He tears the package open with his teeth and then works quickly to roll the condom down his thick shaft.

He positions himself at my entrance as he kisses my lips. I gasp as he bites my lower lip, grabs my hips, and shoves the head of his cock inside me.

Tyler's groan echoes around the room. "Fuck, Avery. God. I already want to come."

His fingers dig into my hips as he pushes in and out of me. The feel of him inside me, stretching me, is just about enough to send me over the edge for the second time.

"I've missed you so much," Tyler pants as he pumps faster and faster. I grab a fistful of his hair. "I've missed you, too."

A low growl emits from the back of his throat as he bites his lip in ecstasy as he finds his own release. A shudder ripples through his body as he leans his forehead against mine while he attempts to catch his breath.

A content sigh leaves his mouth after he kisses my lips one more time. His nose skims across my jawline. "That was . . . wow."

I laugh as I play with a wild hair that's poking up from the top of his head. "I agree. But it has been a long time for me, so I really don't have anything to compare it to."

He raises his eyebrow. "How long has it been?"

My mouth runs dry as I'm about to admit how lame my life has been in the sex department. "Three years."

"Are you saying I was the last man you've been with?"

I nod. "Yes. I never met anyone that I thought was worth bringing into Maddie's life, so I kept to myself. Between taking care of Maddie and running the bar, I didn't have much time for much else anyway."

Tyler's thumb runs over my cheek. "I'm sorry for not coming back sooner."

"You're here now," I whisper.

Tyler smiles. "I swear from here on out I'll do right by you, Avery. I promise to be a better man for you and Maddie." Tyler traces my cheek with the pad of his thumb. "I love you, Avery."

I melt at the sound of his words and I pray that things work out for us this time because it will absolutely crush me if they don't.

I touch his face as I stare into his eyes. "I love you, too."

He bites his bottom lip before he crushes his mouth to mine. Tyler's erection slides up against me and I smile, knowing that we're about to make love yet one more time.

Once we're nearly exhausted from two rounds, we decide since there's no sign of Blake in the bar that we'll check back over at his place.

"His car is still parked in the exact same spot," Tyler says.

"Maybe we should call the police," I suggest.

"They won't do anything. I learned that from when our band's front man went missing. The cops won't get involved until the person has been missing over seventy-two hours."

"Three days? What if he's lying in a ditch hurt somewhere, waiting for help, but because of the stupid three-day-rule shit, he doesn't make it."

"It's crazy. Trust me, I know, but I'm afraid we have to keep looking on our own until then. It's late tonight. We'll check inside and if he's not in the house, in the morning we'll go over to his parents' house."

"Good plan," I agree.

When we find him I'm going to give him a piece of my mind for causing all this worry.

TYLER

We head to Blake's place, and minus the fact that I'm worrying my ass off about my best friend's safety, I'm still on cloud nine.

Never in my hopes of all hopes did I envision a reunion with Avery to be like this. When I came here, I expected a good slap in the face from her. Instead, she's given me two precious gifts: Her heart and a beautiful daughter.

I've always heard people say they fell in love the moment they laid eyes on their kid for the first time, but I never really believed that to be true . . . until now, that is.

Sure, I was blindsided by the fact that I have a child, but it didn't stop me from loving her instantly. I know Avery and I have been apart a long time, but there's no doubt in my mind that Maddie is my daughter. She looks so much like me. We have the same blue eyes, blond hair, and I even noticed we share the same crooked smile. She's so sweet, and perfect, and hearing her call me Daddy lights up my entire world.

When we pull up to Blake's, the Mustang is still parked out front. I turn toward Avery and tell her, "See. It hasn't moved in two days."

"Let's get inside and take another look around."

We get out and walk up onto the porch and I twist the knob on the door, but it doesn't open. "Shit. It's locked."

Avery frowns. "Maybe he left the back open."

I nod and then lead the way off the porch and around the side of the house. The gate leading into Blake's backyard is open, so I slip inside the fence with no problem. I'm about to turn the corner to check the back door when something I spot out of the corner of my eye causes me to stop dead in my tracks.

"Stay where you are, Avery," I order with my back toward her, stopping her from coming any farther into the yard.

"What?" she asks, clearly confused.

I dig in my pocket for my cell, and then search for the flashlight feature. The moment it snaps on, I gasp like all the wind has just been knocked out of me.

Blake's lying on the ground, still wearing the clothes he had on two nights ago, and my body instantly goes into panic mode. "Oh, shit! Blake!"

I scream his name and run to him. I fall to my knees at his side and take in the scene before me. Blake's face is covered in blood, and the flesh around his eyes is so swollen that it's hard to even recognize him. He's taken a much more severe beating than what he was given at the bar. Sure he was banged up, but it was nothing like this.

"Oh, my God! Blake! Is he all right? Oh, my God." Avery's panicked words smash into my ears as she races to my side. "Is he . . . Did you . . . Oh, God."

I reach out and touch the side of his neck with two fingers, hoping to find a pulse. Relief floods me when his skin is warm to the touch and I detect a faint pulse.

"He's alive, but he's really hurt. He needs an ambulance," I say.

Avery grabs her cell and dials 9-1-1, explains the situation, and runs out front to get Blake's house number for the operator.

While she does that, I stare down at my friend and wish there was something I could do for him. I feel so helpless just sitting by him without being able to do anything.

I touch his arm and try to do the only thing I can by comforting him. "You're going to be all right. Hang in there, buddy."

Sirens wail all around as an ambulance and police cars arrive at the scene. The paramedics work quickly to move me out of the way and then get right to work on Blake.

They try to talk to him, but he never responds. One of the guys holds open his eyelids and shines a light in his eyes while another pulls out a needle and pokes it into Blake's skin to start an IV.

Avery clings to my side and presses her face against my shoulder. It's hard to watch them work on him and it hits me that this may be the last time I see my friend alive if they can't help him get better. Watching Blake fight for his life opens the floodgates to a lot of still-healing memories.

"Avery?" The same cop from the bar the other night approaches us and removes his hat. "I know this is a difficult time for you, but I need to ask the two of you some questions so we can get a handle on what's happened here."

Avery nods. "Anything. I want to help find whoever did this."

Officer Ryder pulls out a notepad and says, "How did you discover the victim?"

"When we came to check on him, the front door was locked, so we thought we'd try the back, and that's when we found him."

The cop nods. "What made you come check on him?"

This time I feel that I need to speak up.

I clear my throat. "I stayed here two nights ago, but I hadn't seen him since the fight at the bar. When he didn't return my calls, I started to worry."

He makes a few notes on the paper. "Do you have any idea what happened to him and why he's out in his backyard like this?"

I shake my head. "No, but I did notice he's wearing the same clothes as the last time I saw him."

"Oh, God," Avery interjects. "Do you think the guys from the bar that night followed him home? That's the only logical explanation, and they're the only people that I can think of who would want to harm Blake."

"It's highly likely that's exactly what has happened," the officer says. "Which is why I'm going to put out an APB on the men who had the confrontation with him the other night. Those men are known problems in this town, which is why I wish Blake would've pressed charges when he could before. Having incidents on record is always helpful, especially when a situation like this arises. It gives us a clear picture most of the time on who we need to start with in our line of questioning. There's no doubt that whoever did this to Blake didn't intend for him to live to identify them, which is why it is of utmost importance to find these guys and get them off the streets. If they aren't afraid to do this kind of crime and hurt someone like this, they won't give it a second thought when they do it again."

"I'll do anything I can to help, officer," I tell the man. "Just tell me what needs to be done."

He frowns. "There's not much that you can do but sit back and let us do our jobs. We'll find them and bring them to justice. If you think of anything else, let us know."

Officer Ryder squeezes the button on the side of the walkie-talkie that's strapped to his shoulder and says, "We need an APB on Jerry Rose, Thomas Hersel, and Larry Deitz. All known to be associated with the organized gang the Outlaws."

The radio buzzes to life. "Copy that."

The paramedics work quickly to get Blake on a backboard and then put him on a stretcher. A white plastic neck brace is also strapped on him to stabilize his head and prevent it from moving around.

Avery turns into me, tears flowing from her eyes. "I can't believe this is happening."

I wrap my arm around her shoulder and pull her in tight against me. I wish I could tell her that Blake's fine, though the truth is, I'm worried about him myself. But at least now Avery and I have each other and we can get through this together.

AVERY

It's been close to five hours since they brought Blake into the hospital and he hasn't woken up yet. All the testing they did on him revealed a slight brain bleed but the doctors think it's not enough to cause significant swelling to the point where they would need to operate. They're hoping his body will simply reabsorb the blood and the swelling will reduce on its own.

I sit at Blake's bedside and hold his hand in mine while Tyler sits next to me. Being here reminds me of being at Granny's bedside after the fire years ago. It's difficult to witness someone you care about struggle with so much pain. I pray Blake's outcome is better than my father's was and that whatever happens, Tyler can handle it and won't take off running like he did the last time when things got hard.

We haven't left the hospital since they brought Blake in. Blake's mom stopped in to see him, but she didn't stay long. It was the first time I'd ever met the woman in the time I've known Blake. He doesn't talk much about her—just says that they aren't that close.

I check the clock on the wall, and it's nearly eight in the morning. It's almost time for Maddie to get up, so we're going to have to decide how much longer we stay here because Maddie will be asking for me before long.

I called Granny last night to make sure she was okay watching Maddie all night, and of course she told me that it was no problem. Granny loves spending time with her great-granddaughter.

Tyler rubs smooth circles on my back. "Tired?"

"Yes," I say and then scrub my hand down my face. "I don't want Blake to be alone when he wakes up, but I think I need to get home to Maddie soon."

Tyler fishes his keys from his front pocket. "Take the car and go home and rest."

"What about you?" I ask.

"I'll be fine. Come back and get me in a few hours."

I stare into Tyler's eyes, and all I see is how caring and loving he is. He's been amazing with Maddie and I know if I allow myself, I could fall madly in love with him very quickly.

I don't know how I'm going to feel when they find that singer in his band and he has to go back on the road. It'll crush me and I'm sure now that Maddie knows him, she'll have a bunch of questions of her own when he's no longer around a lot.

Just as I'm about to stand up, Blake's fingers twitch in my grasp and I immediately freeze in place. "Blake? Can you hear me?"

They twitch again and I reach for the call button attached to the side of the bed to alert the staff that we need a nurse.

There's a knock at the door and the petite, dark-haired nurse who's on duty enters the room. "You needed something?"

"Yes!" I say and I can hear the excitement in my own voice. "He's moving!"

She rushes over to his bedside and pulls a penlight from the front pocket of her scrubs. She lifts Blake's eyelids and shines the light in his eyes one at a time. "Blake, I'm Anna, your nurse. I'm going to grab your hand. Give it a squeeze if you can hear me." She takes the hand opposite of the one I'm holding and says to him, "That's me touching you. Squeeze back if you can. Let me know that you can hear me."

We wait with bated breath, but then something magical happens. Blake's fingers twitch on the other hand and he squeezes not only the nurse's hand but mine too.

"Good, Blake," the nurse says and then leans over to adjust the IV tubing attached to him.

"You're hot." Blake's scratchy voice comes out barely over a whisper.

The nurse's cheeks turn a deep shade of red. "It looks like someone is starting to feel better."

"How are you feeling?" I ask Blake. "Is there anything I can get you?"

"Her phone number would make me feel a lot better."

Tyler chuckles beside me. "And he's back."

The woman assesses Blake's physical condition, all the while fending off his advances with smiles and shakes of her head. It's obvious that this brain bleed isn't going to keep him down for long.

When she's through, the nurse smiles and addresses Blake directly. "Okay, try to take it easy. I'm going to alert your doctor that you're awake. He'll want to talk to you right away."

"Okay."

"Use the call light if you need me for anything," she reminds him.

His eyebrow tweaks up and even though the swelling hides most of the expression on his face, it's clear to see that his brain is thinking up some typical Blake ornery things to say. "You mean, when I want you, all I have to do is press this button and you'll come to my room? Sweet. I need to talk to someone about getting one of these things installed at my house. I'd love to have you as my beck-and-call girl."

She rolls her eyes. "Rest, and only the button if you need me for something pertaining to your health."

"Sex is very much a part of a person's overall health," he argues.

The nurse gives him a pointed look and then leaves the room. Clearly she's not going to fall for Blake's bullshit.

As soon as the door shuts, Blake sighs. "She totally wants me."

Tyler and I laugh in unison, and my heart is happy now that my friend is okay.

"It's good to see the two of you together again. Did you finally let him meet Maddie?" Blake asks and I nod. "Good. I never felt right about keeping it secret, but it wasn't my business to tell him about her. That was between the two of you."

"Thank you, Blake. You're a good friend."

"Does Maddie have you wrapped around her cute little finger yet, Tyler?"

My gaze flicks over to Tyler and he nods. "She does. I'm such a goner when it comes to that girl."

Blake grins. "I knew she would. She's too adorable for a person to not fall in love with her the moment they see her. You'll be a good dad."

"Thanks, man. I'm sure going to try. I've got a lot of making up to do—" Tyler reaches over and threads his fingers through mine. "—with both of them. I'm going to do right by them."

Blake nods. "I know you will."

We sit there for a moment, and then finally Tyler asks, "What the hell happened to you? Did those dudes from the bar that night do this to you?"

He sighs. "Yeah. Those assholes must've followed me home from the bar, because they totally caught me off guard. I was unlocking the house and then boom: I was knocked out cold from behind. The next thing I knew they were dragging me around back where they finished beating my ass as one big group."

"Shit, man. I'm sorry I wasn't with you."

Blake shakes his head. "Are you crazy? You'd probably be in the bed right next to me if they'd snuck up on us both, and Avery would be here holding both our hands."

"You're probably right. All the same, I'm still sorry."

"Don't lose one night of sleep over it, man. I'll be fine."

Another knock on the door sounds and then Officer Ryder walks in the door with a stack of papers in his hands. "How are you guys doing? I heard from the nurse Blake was awake in here, so I thought it would be a good time to come in and take a report from him about what actually happened. Did you get a good look at your attacker's face or faces?"

Blake turns toward me. "Can you help me sit this bed up a little?"

I press the button and his head rises up. "Better?"

He nods and then slowly turns his attention back to Officer Ryder. "I did. It was those same douches from the bar that we got into it with earlier that night. The three of them attacked me as I was going into my house."

"Did any one of them specifically do this or did they all three have their hands on you?"

"All three," he confirms. "Worst thing is they were smiling and fucking enjoying themselves. It made me sick."

The cop makes a few notes and then says, "This isn't the first time we've had problems with these guys, but it is the first time someone has been brave enough to identify them in a crime and then stick by it. These guys like to hurt people. They get off on it, so I'm going to do everything within my power to make sure these guys pay for their crimes against you. We've already got them in custody and will proceed with criminal charges now that you've been able to identify them."

"Thank you," Blake says. "You let me know what you need from me, and consider it done. I don't want these pricks doing this to someone else—someone who might not be as lucky as I was."

"Will do. Take care of yourself." Officer Ryder turns toward me and smiles. "See you around, Avery."

Tyler's fingers curl around the armrest of the chair and as soon as the cop leaves, he says, "That guy has a thing for you."

"What? No, he doesn't," I quip. "He's just being friendly and doing his job."

"Well, I don't like it. I don't like the idea of him sniffing around you when I'm gone."

His admission of jealousy catches me off guard. "Tyler, if this is going to work, then you're going to have to trust me. We'll be spending a lot of time apart, so trust is going to be crucial in our relationship."

Tyler sighs deeply and then scrubs his hand down his face. "I know. I'm sorry. I don't mean to sounds like . . ."

"A jealous stalker boyfriend," Blake adds in for him.

Tyler gives him a pointed look. "Yes, that."

"No problem, dude. But seriously, Avery's a good girl. I don't think you'd have to worry about her running around on you. She's—"

"Blake," I cut him off, stopping him midsentence. "I know you're trying to help me, but Tyler and me . . . we got this."

He gives me a sheepish grin. "Sorry. Continue."

Tyler grabs my hand and stands up. "Let's go talk."

"Oh, come on, guys. You can't take away my entertainment," Blake complains.

I laugh as Tyler pulls me toward the door.

We walk hand in hand through the hospital, and I'm not sure what's on Tyler's mind, but there's a worried expression on his face. It seems that whatever he wants to talk about is pretty damn serious.

TYLER

When we reach the parking lot, I turn to face Avery. "There's something that's been weighing on my mind all night and I think we need to talk about it."

Her brow furrows. "Okay. I'm all ears. What's up?"

I lick my suddenly dry lips. "I don't want to go back on tour with my band."

Since I met Maddie the other day, the thought of leaving this town hurts like hell. Maddie instantly stole my heart and made me realize that music should not control my life. I can be a musician anywhere. The music is in me, and I'll never lose that, even if I follow my heart and chase a new dream.

It's the choices I made that led me to Wicked White even though my heart really isn't into the kind of music that we perform. I want to make music that speaks my truth, and in order to create that kind of music, I have to start with being honest with myself and going after what my heart truly wants. Right now that's to be a family with Avery and Maddie. Nothing else matters to me but them.

Shock passes over her face. I'm sure the admission I just made isn't one that she expected to hear. "What makes you say that? I thought music was your life."

"It was," I say and then pause. "Growing up, all I ever dreamed about doing was being a musician. Creating music and performing has been one hundred percent what my life has been about. There was nothing that mattered more to me. My dad knew that, which is why he pushed me so hard to get out of this town. He knew that a career as a performer would never be anything more for me than just a dream if I got trapped in the small-town life. He didn't want to see me get tied down like he did. He loved to tell me stories about all the big dreams he had growing up, and when I asked him why he never tried to make them come true, he would always just tell me that things changed for him when he met my mother—that she became the most important thing to him. They got married. He got a job at a local factory and then they had me.

"For some reason he never thought his simple life was good enough for me. He never wanted to see me settle for anything less than my dreams, so he pushed me. He pushed me to be better—to want to get out of this town. Dad's biggest fear was that I would get a girl pregnant and get trapped here in this town, which is why I think he made me make that promise to him."

"There's nothing wrong with wanting your child to accomplish more than you did," Avery says. "I can see why he would push you like that. I want the same for Maddie. He wanted you to have the best life you can."

I take her hand in mine. "That's where I think he was wrong though, Avery. When he told me to go out and find my dream, I don't think he could've ever possibly known that my dream was going to come into this town and find me."

"What are you saying, Tyler?" she whispers.

I trace her cheek with the tips of my fingers. "I'm saying that my dreams have changed, and if I'm to keep my promise to my dad, then I need to go after them. My dream is you, Avery. You and Maddie. I want us to be a family."

"I told you we'd give us a shot," she says.

Instantly, I shake my head. "I don't want to be away from you and I don't want to miss a single day in Maddie's life. I've missed too many firsts already that I'll never get back. I love you, Avery. You and Maddie. I don't want to see you just part-time or the times when I'm not on the road or in the studio—I want the two of you in my life every day."

"I can't just pack up and leave here, Tyler. I've worked hard to make this a home for Maddie and me. I've got the bar and Granny—my life is here."

"I know," I tell her to try and alleviate some of the confusion and panic I see in her eyes. "I'm going to come to you."

"You can't do music from here."

"I know and I don't care. None of that matters now."

Tears fill her eyes. "You can't be serious. You can't leave everything you've worked for on a whim."

I cradle her face in my hands and force her to look into my eyes. I want her to know that I'm being a thousand percent serious. "This isn't a whim. I regretted leaving you here the moment I did it three years ago. I wanted to come back and beg your forgiveness so many times, but I was afraid—afraid of confronting my guilt. I want you now and forever. I promise you my heart from this moment forward. It's yours for the taking. All you have to do is tell me that you want me to stay. I need to hear that you need me just as much as I need you if I'm going to walk away from everything."

"Tyler," she says my name through a strained voice and I can tell it's taking everything inside her to hold back from sobbing. "I want you, but I don't want you to resent me or Maddie down the road."

"I will never do that. I swear it. The band—it's not much to give up. I'm not happy there. No one gets along, so I couldn't care less if I ever see those guys again. If music is meant to happen for me, it will happen in a way that you and Maddie can still be a part of my everyday world.

"Say yes, Avery. Say that you're in this with me."

She closes her eyes. "Of course I am."

I crush my lips to hers. Avery—she's my destiny. There are too many times fate has brought us together, and I can no longer deny that she is my dream and this is exactly where I'm supposed to be.

Epilogue

THREE YEARS LATER . . .

AVERY

Sitting offstage with Maddie while she watches her daddy's every move on stage is always the best seat in the house. When Tyler first told me he was giving up music to be with me and Maddie, I was scared. It worried me that he would miss this business and crave it to the point where he would leave us behind to find it again, but now I know that I shouldn't have been afraid. I had nothing to fear.

Tyler did just what he promised. He's made Maddie and me a part of his everyday life.

The day that Ace White was found, Tyler had to go back to California to officially quit and see if he could get out of his contract. It was surprisingly easy for Tyler to get out of the band since they only utilized his talents as a drummer and the band went through a bit of restructuring. There was an industry executive at Mopar Records who took a special interest in Tyler and his reasons for wanting to quit. He saw something in Tyler—something he thought would resonate with fans—and when he asked Tyler what genre of music really called to him, Tyler, of course, said country music—the stuff he was born and raised on.

Now, three years later we're sitting at his sold-out tour for promoting his first solo record. Tyler Mercer has made it to the big time on his own terms.

He flew out to a studio in California for a couple weeks to finish his album, so he wasn't gone long. He's made it a point to tell the record label that he'll only tour during the summer months once Maddie starts school next year because he likes having his family on the road with him.

It's funny how sometimes in life if you step out and take a chance, things have a way of working themselves out.

"This next song goes out to my little girl, Maddie." Tyler's voice cuts through the arena. "If it's all right with you all, I'd like to bring her out here on stage so I can sing it to her. It's called 'Daddy's Angel.'"

The crowd erupts in applause. This particular song was number one on the charts for nearly six weeks. It really resonates with people because the lyrics are a heartfelt story about the love a father has for his daughter. People can connect with something that's true.

Tyler walks over to us and picks Maddie up, and then he wraps his arm around me and kisses my lips. "I'll bring her right back, Mom."

I giggle and shake my head at his silliness as Tyler leads our daughter out on stage with him. She's five now, and growing so fast. I'm glad Tyler's been in her life the last few years. He was right. If he'd been out on the road a lot during these last three years, he would've missed so much in her life. The two of them are inseparable now. Her daddy is her world and she's the apple of Tyler's eye.

A collective sound of *awww* comes from the crowd as they spot Tyler holding Maddie. He walks up to the microphone and asks Maddie if she's going to help him sing this time.

"Of course I will, Daddy. It's my favorite song since it's about me."

That gives the crowd a good chuckle. Kids say the darndest things and they are always so brutally honest.

Tyler turns toward his band. "Start us off, guys."

The music plays and Tyler comes in on cue and sings the first verse of the song. It's basically the story of our life. How we met, and how we have the most perfect little girl in the world, and how once he found her he decided he wasn't going to let her go.

The chorus comes into play and Maddie and Tyler lean in and sing into the microphone together. Her little voice rings around the arena and her bravery makes me smile.

It's the most precious thing I've ever seen—the two greatest loves of my life just being together—and I thank God every day for blessing me with them.

Had it not been for Maddie coming into my life when she did, I don't know what I would've done. I was in a dark place, but she gave me hope—a reason to keep being strong and fight my way back into the light.

The last few beats of the song play out and then the crowd erupts in another round of applause. Maddie has a smile on her face that stretches from ear to ear. I can see her loving this life just as much as Tyler does, and it wouldn't surprise me that when she grows up, she'll want to be a singer just like him.

"Everyone give it up for my baby girl, Maddie!" Tyler calls for another round of applause and then whispers in her ear and she immediately waves to the crowd as he sets her down. Tyler points toward me and she comes barreling back in my direction.

"Hey, sweetie! That was great!" I praise her.

"Thanks, Mommy. I love it when Daddy lets me sing with him." The smile she's still wearing is infectious.

"He loves it too," I tell her. "He thinks you've got a great voice."

"I know," she says. "He already told me that."

I chuckle, and Maddie and I stand there and wait for Tyler to finish his set.

He plays a couple more songs and then he thanks his fans for coming out to see his show before he runs off stage and into my waiting arms. "That was so great, babe."

"Thanks! I think the real star of the show tonight was a certain little lady," Tyler says as he bends down and scoops Maddie back up into his arms.

I laugh. "Soon she's going to be too big for you to carry around like that all the time."

"Never," he says. "She'll always be my little girl, even when she's grown up and married."

"Ewww," Maddie says. "Boys are yucky. Except for you, Daddy."

Tyler laughs. "That's what I like to hear, just remember that when you turn about fourteen and you ask me when you're allowed to go on dates."

Tyler hooks his arm around me. "Speaking of dates . . . did you take it?"

I nod. "I did."

"Well?! What was the result? I've been dying to know."

I give him a knowing smile. "There were two little pink lines, so it looks like you're going to be a daddy again."

Tyler's face lights up and you'd think I just told him he'd been given a million dollars. He's the most excited that I've ever seen him. He leans in and plants his lips on mine. "Just when I think things can't get any better in my life, you find a way to blow my mind by doing something awesome."

I laugh. "I think it was more than just me that made this happen, so I can't take all the credit."

"That's true. My super sperm just loves to knock you up. I think since we're so good at it we should plan for another baby right after this one is born. I want a huge family. Eight or nine kids has a nice ring to it, doesn't it?"

I pat his chest. "Whoa. Slow down. We're not farmers in need of a bazillion kids. I think two, maybe three, will be plenty."

"We'll have to see about that. I'd love to have a house full of kids. I mean, hell, look at Maddie. She's amazing. We might as well grace the world with a little more of that awesomeness."

I loop my arm around his waist. "We'll see about that. For now let's just take it one kid at a time. Okay?"

He kisses the top of my head. "Deal, but can we at least practice making number three?"

I bite my lower lip. "Practice does make perfect."

He kisses me one more time. "I love you, Avery."

"I love you too," I reply without any second thoughts because I know this man is my destiny and no matter what life throws at us, we'll handle it together.

ACKNOWLEDGMENTS

The first person I want to thank is you, my dear readers, for giving this series a shot! Even though I could never thank all of you in person, I hope you know how much I appreciate each and every one of you.

Jennifer Wolfel, I seriously don't know how I could ever write a story without your input. Your love, support, and never-wavering faith in me and my work truly means the world to me. Thank you for being your amazing self.

Emily Snow and Holly Malgieri, thank you all for being there for me over the years. I treasure the friendship I have with each of you so much!

Jill Marsal, thank you for being an amazing agent!

Charlotte Herscher, thank you for being an amazing editor and working so hard on my last few projects! You totally get me and my books and I couldn't have asked for a better person to work with on the Wicked White series.

To my awesome team at Montlake, you guys are wicked awesome!

My beautiful ladies in Valentine's Vixens Group, you all are the best. You guys always brighten my day and push me to be a better writer. Thank you!

To the romance blogging community, thank you for always supporting me and my books. I can't tell you how much every share, tweet, post, and comment means to me. I read them all, and every time I feel giddy. THANK YOU for everything you do. Blogging is not an easy job, and I can't tell you how much I appreciate what you do for indie authors like me. You totally make our world go round.

Last, but always first in my life, my husband and son: thank you for putting up with me. I love you both more than words can express.

ABOUT THE AUTHOR

New York Times and *USA Today* best-selling author Michelle A. Valentine is a self-professed music addict who resides in Columbus, Ohio, with her husband, son, and two scrappy dogs. When she's not slaving away over her next novel, she enjoys expressing herself with off-the-wall crafts and trying her hand at party planning.

While in college, Michelle's first grown-up job was in a medical office, where she decided she loved working with people so much she changed her major from drafting and design to nursing. It wasn't until her toddler son occupied the television constantly that she discovered the amazing world of romance novels. Soon after reading over 180 books in a year, she decided to dive into trying her own hand at writing her first novel, and she hasn't looked back. After years of rejection, in 2012 she self-published *Rock the Heart*, her tenth full-length novel, and it hit the *New York Times* bestsellers list. Her subsequent books have gone on to list multiple times on both the *New York Times* and *USA Today* bestseller lists.

10-16

Michelle loves to hear from her readers!
To contact Michelle:
E-mail: michelleavalentinebooks@gmail.com
Website: www.michelleavalentine.com
Facebook: www.facebook.com/AuthorMichelleAValentine